A Moment to Remember

A Moment to Remember

Nina Lambert

PIATKUS

First published in Great Britain in 1989 by
Judy Piatkus (Publishers) Ltd of
5 Windmill Street, London W1

British Library Cataloguing in Publication Data

Lambert, Nina
    A moment to remember.
    I. Title
    823'.914[F]

    ISBN 0-86188-782-4

Phototypeset in 11/12pt Compugraphic Times by
Action Typesetting Limited, Gloucester
Printed and bound in Great Britain by
Mackays of Chatham PLC, Chatham, Kent

Chapter One

Lisa Campbell lifted the soufflé proudly out of the oven. Beautifully risen, golden-crusted, it looked just like the picture in the recipe book.

'How many calories?' queried her flat-mate, unappreciatively. Sarah was a fashion model and was permanently on a diet. Lisa, more generously proportioned than her friend, spooned out her creation on to Sarah's plate and proffered her the salad bowl.

'Don't be discouraging, Sarah,' she pleaded. 'I've got to have someone to practise on.'

'I just wish it didn't always have to be me,' complained Sarah churlishly. 'I've put on three pounds since you moved in. Gosh, this is divine,' she continued, succumbing mournfully to temptation.

Lisa beamed with satisfaction. Anything that could undermine Sarah's iron control over her appetite had to be a gastronomic triumph – although Lisa should not have needed this reassurance, having just completed the first term of a professional cookery course with flying colours.

She had worked hard. She badly needed the copper-bottomed credentials that her eventual diploma would give her. She had reached the age of twenty-one without gaining any proper qualifications and her numerous jobs

1

had tended to last a disappointingly short time. Jobs were not easy to come by back home in Auchterbrae, and despite Lisa's bold commutes in her ancient jalopy to Inverness and back each day, her forays had not led her any nearer a respectable career. And so she had come to London to seek her fortune.

She was more at home in the kitchen than in the office. Her spelling was logical rather than accurate, her typewriters had proved unco-operative, and she had an unfailing knack for pulling the wrong plugs out of switchboards, usually when the boss was about to clinch a deal. Had she been as sweet, docile and helpless as her incompetence suggested, her employers might have indulged her hapless femininity. But Lisa was cursed with the heritage of her Campbell blood — naturally volatile, she disliked being talked down to, and had an unfortunate tendency to answer back. So although she would put herself out willingly if asked nicely, and honestly tried to do her best, she reacted fierily to sarcasm, rudeness or impatience, and invariably managed to pre-empt dismissal by resigning, head held high, before she received the inevitable marching orders.

Her father, a harassed country doctor, took solace in the knowledge that Lisa, a superb cook and housekeeper, who generated the same warmth about the home as her mother had done before her, was surely destined to make some lucky man an admirable wife, and was likely to be snapped up before she was very much older.

Lisa nurtured no such cosy ideas about her future. She chafed at her restricted life, she craved wider horizons, excitement, adventure. She found the local talent, lads she had grown up with, tame, narrow-minded and boring. Generous-hearted, she spared their feelings as much as she was able. She wouldn't have wanted them to realise how tedious she found their attentions. She was

2

fed up hearing them rave about her looks, which to her mind were totally unsatisfactory. Lisa would have loved to be a tall, thin, olive-skinned, dark-eyed beauty. Instead she was, to her chagrin, small-boned, ample-bosomed, green-eyed, red-haired and pale-complexioned. If you had told her, romantically, that her hair glowed with amber lights, her eyes shone with sorcery, and her figure brought out the worst in men — she would have snorted in derision.

'Another piece of pie, Father?' she coaxed one evening, while Dr Campbell was contentedly digesting a succession of his favourite dishes, which Lisa had cooked to perfection.

Her father picked up the wheedling tone which she had inherited so accurately from her mother.

'Right you are, my girl,' he sighed gruffly. 'You've softened me up nicely. What is it this time? Have you been and got the sack from Archie McTay? I knew fine you'd never hit it off with that dragon Fiona.'

Lisa smiled sweetly. She was currently working as a typist at an agricultural feed merchant's. Fiona Sinclair was the senior female employee, locally renowned as a battleaxe. Lisa was, as it happened, getting on exceedingly well with the dreaded Fiona, who regarded Lisa, the doctor's daughter, as a handy diagnostician for her numerous aches and pains.

'Away you go,' scolded Lisa, removing the pie to the larder. 'Mr McTay thinks the world of me. If I stay ten years, I'll be taking over when Fiona retires. Unless . . .' She poured his coffee and announced innocently, 'I shall be twenty-one in April.'

'No need to start dropping hints already,' growled Dr Campbell. 'It's not Christmas yet.'

'What I mean is, I inherit my mother's money, do I not?'

Mrs Campbell had been a thrifty woman, and had saved religiously for her daughter's bottom drawer. The savings were sacrosanct until Lisa's marriage or twenty-first birthday, whichever came first.

'That's correct. And let me remind you, Lisa, your mother didn't put by all those years just for you to fritter it. It's for when you've got a home of your own.'

Lisa fetched some papers from the sideboard and handed them to her father wordlessly, her green eyes bright with persuasion.

'A cookery course,' muttered her father uncertainly. 'In London? Could you not do one of these in Edinburgh, Lisa? It would surely be cheaper.'

'Father, this is one of the most famous cookery schools in the world. With a diploma from them, I'd be employable anywhere. Mother's money would pay the fees, with a good bit over, and I can earn extra money doing private catering at weekends and holidays. There's a big demand for that kind of thing in London. Eventually I want to set up my own business. I've got so many ideas. Cookery's the one thing I'm really good at. Imagine learning how to make all the classic French dishes − filet de boeuf en croûte, cassoulet, ratatouille, bouillabaisse . . .' The French words rolled seductively off her tongue. 'I'd make you so proud of me, Father.'

'And where would you live?' queried Dr Campbell sternly. 'London's no place for a young lass on her own.'

Lisa sighed. She had known this would be the big stumbling block. Dr Campbell was a confirmed Puritan. He vetted all her boyfriends, innocuous though they were, with a beady eye. Naturally he would think that in London practised seducers lurked in every doorway. He gave her a long, unyielding look.

'If you promise not to pester the life out of me,' he grunted, finally, 'I'll be making a few enquiries.'

In a moment of weakness, Lisa had agreed to a date that evening with one of her more persistent admirers, Douglas, who was articled to a solicitor in Inverness and considered to be highly eligible. He was very attentive throughout dinner, a candlelit affair at a local roadhouse. Lisa didn't rate the food very highly. It made her all the more confident that once she got her qualifications she would take the catering world by storm.

On the way home, Douglas parked the car purposefully in a country lane and set about kissing Lisa very thoroughly. Lisa squirmed uncomfortably. Douglas always got himself terribly excited, she couldn't for the life of her understand why. His hands, predictably, started to wander. She pushed them firmly away. Evenings with Douglas always followed this inevitable pattern.

'Och, Lisa,' he groaned, exasperated. 'You shouldn't have encouraged me!'

'I did not encourage you,' she retorted primly. 'We've been all through this before. I only agreed to come because you promised to be good. Besides, there's no point in getting serious. I'll be away to London shortly.'

'To London? And what, may I ask, will you be doing there?'

'I'm going to qualify as a professional cook,' Lisa informed him grandly.

'And find yourself a rich husband while you're about it, I suppose,' remarked Douglas caustically.

'I've got no intentions of getting married at the moment. After I've qualified, I shall be setting up my own catering business.'

Douglas began laughing unmercifully. Lisa was not amused.

'Like everyone else, Douglas,' said Lisa, green eyes flashing, 'you underestimate me.'

Douglas stroked her cheek gently with his finger.

'To be sure I don't, Lisa. Somewhere beneath that tough skin of yours there beats a heart of stone. And one day some brave man's going to dynamite it. Good luck to him, I say.' He started the engine with an air of resignation. 'And to you, Lisa, my sweet.'

A few days later, Dr Campbell solemnly handed Lisa a Building Society book and an envelope containing a cheque.

'I've been making enquiries,' he began grimly, 'down in London. I recalled Alistair Forsyth has a daughter about your age. He and I were at St Andrew's together, and he's now a specialist in Harley Street. I contacted him to ask his advice about where a young girl might be safe living alone in London. He told me that his daughter's flat-mate had just got married and that Sarah was in need of someone *sensible* ,' and he gave a particular emphasis to the word, 'to take her place. I'd feel a lot happier, Lisa, if you were not amongst complete strangers. Any daughter of Alistair's must be well brought up, I don't doubt. He suggested that you telephone her. Here's the number. And mind you do it on the cheap rate.'

And with this bombshell he went off to take his morning surgery.

Lisa was even more distracted than usual that day as she went about her duties at McTay's Feedstuffs. She could hardly wait for six p.m., but there was, unfortunately, no answer from Sarah Forsyth's telephone. She rang every half-hour until a despairing half-past eleven, when at last, sitting tensely by the phone in her pyjamas with her third cup of cocoa, Lisa heard a husky voice drawl, 'Hello?'

'Would that be Sarah Forsyth?' asked Lisa eagerly. 'This is Lisa Campbell, Andrew Campbell's daughter, your father's friend, you know. He would have told you

6

I'd be ringing. I'm coming to live in London shortly and I was hoping to share your flat.'

A merry peal of laughter greeted this forthright approach.

'Oh yes,' Sarah's languid tones confirmed. 'I gather our daddies seem to think we're suitable chaperones for each other.' She laughed again, skittishly, and Lisa fancied she could hear a deeper male chuckle somewhere in the background.

'I was thinking of coming down next Friday,' continued Lisa doggedly, determined to make some firm arrangement. 'Would that be convenient with you?'

'Of course, darling. I've got no choice. As my father's as worried about me as yours is about you, let's put both their sweet little minds at rest, shall we?' Sarah seemed to find the whole situation mildly hilarious. 'Listen, Lisa, I probably won't be in, but the caretaker has a spare key. Just get him to let you in and have a good look round. You'd be having the smaller bedroom – the one with the single bed.' From the way Sarah was giggling, Lisa thought that someone must be tickling her. She didn't appear to be taking the conversation at all seriously. 'Flat D, 63 Rochester Terrace, that's near Earl's Court, okay? Must go now. Byee.'

Lisa was mightily glad that her father had not overheard this exchange, or he might have had a few misgivings about Sarah's suitability as a mentor for his daughter. All that now remained was for her to secure an interview at the cookery school, and then ...

In January 1981, Lisa had taken up her course and duly moved in to Sarah's flat. Everything, so far, had gone strictly according to plan. Now, with one term down and two to go, Lisa aimed to use the Easter vacation to earn a bit of much needed cash. She was convinced that there were plenty of helpless hostesses in London, eager to pay someone else to cope with their dinner parties. The initial problem was going to be making contact with them. Watching Sarah lap up her soufflé, she asked, 'Surely you've got some contacts, Sarah, who'd be willing to give me a try? Can you ask around for me?'

Sarah nibbled thoughtfully on a lettuce leaf.

'Oh, I expect so,' she confirmed airily. 'I don't know anyone who actually *cooks*. I mean, everybody eats out these days, don't they? I suppose they'd find it a lot cheaper, having you in. I'll put the word about.'

'It's not just the money I need,' said Lisa. 'It's the experience. It's a thankless task, cooking for you, what with you always watching your weight.' And with a wicked gleam in her eye, she gave a protesting but defeated Sarah a second delicious helping.

Sarah consumed it guiltily with one eye on her watch.

'Must dash, darling. Richard's meeting me at the ballet. Then we're going on to a party. See you tomorrow,' and she departed, on a cloud of Arpège, leaving Lisa to reflect over the washing-up.

Oh, to be elegant and worldly-wise like Sarah. Hands working automatically, Lisa glared at her reflection in the mirror over the sink – Sarah kept mirrors everywhere – and contemplated her shortcomings. She might have been considered the local siren back home in Auchterbrae, but Douglas and his like had been, it was painfully clear, no connoisseurs of feminine allure. The numerous men who called at the flat for Sarah tended to treat Lisa as Sarah's kid sister, with good reason. She must ask Sarah what she did to her eyes, to make them look so sooty and mysterious. Lisa yearned to look ethereal and was no admirer of her own youthful, healthy glow. She sucked in her cheeks and tried to look haughty, but succeeded only in giving herself a fit of the giggles.

'Good news, darling,' announced Sarah over a starch-reduced breakfast. 'I was telling Richard about your miracle soufflés and so on, and he said "Why doesn't Lisa get in contact with Michael Delaney?" and I thought "Why not?" He and Davina have had this big bust up, you see, and he's got this sort of buffet party fixed up for next Saturday, and now she's walked out he'll have to get caterers in – I mean, I can't see Michael buttering canapés. So if you get in first and give him a buzz, who knows, you might get the job, 'specially as it's such short notice. Richard promised me he'd ring Michael and put in a word for you beforehand. If you pull it off, you could be on your way. It's not just any old party, you know.'

While Lisa interrogated her impatiently, Sarah explained, in her infuriatingly vague and digressive way, that Michael, like Richard, was a freelance photographer, and that the purpose of his party was to entertain the contacts in the media from whom he gained his commissions. Sarah affected shocked amazement that Lisa had never heard of Michael Delaney.

'I mean, he's absolutely brilliant, wildly perfectionist and ruthless with it. I'd give anything to work with him – not that Richard would want me to. Everyone knows Michael's positively lethal with women.'

Richard had recently displaced Sarah's other admirers. A successful fashion photographer, he was no mean catch. Sarah had generously tried to include Lisa in their glamorous social set, but Lisa, knowing when she was out of her depth, had always made excuses and had not been pressed. Although careful not to let it show, Lisa was quite overawed by Richard. Aggressively trendy, he habitually wore hip-hugging jeans and silk shirts open to the waist, revealing the gold medallion nestling in his hairy chest. He and Sarah made a very glamorous couple, although Dr Forsyth, Sarah's father, would have been

9

less than delighted by Richard's reputation as a philanderer.

Lisa was, however, very grateful to Richard for this introduction. This party, she realised, gulping, would be a real challenge. If she could make a good impression at such a gathering, she stood to gain valuable potential clients, vital to her future career as a high-class caterer.

'I'd love to do it,' she assured Sarah, before she had time to get cold feet. 'How do I get in contact with Mr Delaney?'

'Ring him up, silly,' breezed Sarah. 'I even got his number for you. But you'd better move fast, before he hires somebody else. Must fly,' she finished, as a taxi hooted outside the flat, 'I'm late for a session.' And she evaporated gracefully, leaving the usual detritus – a dead Earl Grey teabag, squashed lemon slice, crispbread crumbs, and a half-eaten tub of low-fat yogurt.

Lisa sat, slightly stunned, looking at the piece of paper torn carelessly from Sarah's diary. No time like the present, she told herself. She went boldly to the telephone, picked up the receiver, dialled the first three digits, put it down again, cleared the table, dialled the number properly, got the engaged tone, and drank a strong cup of tea.

Finally, after plucking up sufficient courage to dial the number again, heart hammering as she got through this time, her words of self-introduction died on her lips.

'This is Michael Delaney speaking,' drawled a quiet, cool, deadpan voice. 'I can't talk now, but will call you back. Please leave your message after the tone.'

In panic, she hung up. She had never spoken into an answering machine, and the little speech she had prepared had gone right out of her head. How pathetic, she chided herself. Sarah would have had no difficulty with this. Sarah spent hours on the telephone and was never at a loss for words. 'I'll write it down,' Lisa resolved, sitting down at the kitchen table and chewing the end of a biro with grim determination. A formal statement of her services would always be useful, she could even have cards printed as business expanded. She pondered over her task for some time, and after several discarded attempts, she arrived at the following:

'My name is Lisa Campbell, and I am a professional cook.' (Well, one had to allow oneself a bit of poetic licence.) 'I specialise in private dinner parties and buffets, and can provide any menu you choose within a given budget, plus a fee for my services, which I am sure you will find very reasonable. I use only high quality produce available in season.' And for Michael Delaney's benefit she added, 'Please telephone me to discuss your forth-coming party this Saturday,' and her phone number. Trying to sound efficient, but not too pushy, she rehearsed this speech several times, unaware of the quaint flavour her Highlands accent gave it. Eventually, rather more confidently this time, she picked up the telephone again.

'Hello,' came the familiar voice at the other end of the line, 'Michael Delaney speaking.' Forgetting the routine about waiting for the bleep, Lisa launched straight into her party piece, speaking rather faster than at rehearsal, and thereby giving an unconsciously breathless quality to her voice. After giving her phone number, she sighed with relief, and was just about to hang up when a soft, amused, very male voice said in her ear, 'Trust a woman not to let even an Ansaphone get a word in edgeways.'

She gasped, horror-struck. The real Michael Delaney continued blandly, 'You must have been the click at the end of the tape. Richard's girlfriend's flatmate, I presume, the ultimate in meals on wheels.' His tone was infuriatingly satirical. Lisa chafed at her lack of repartee,

11

and was tempted, in her humiliation, just to hang up. She bit her lip. This would never do as a start to her new career.

'I understand that you'll be needing a catering service this coming Saturday,' she re-stated briskly. 'I happen to be available that night.'

'Mmm. Sounds like an offer I can't refuse,' commented Michael Delaney. There was a pause and a dry chuckle. 'Well then,' he resumed, suddenly businesslike, 'I suggest you come over first, to discuss it – 28 Montpelier Gardens, just off Gloucester Road, near the tube. You can walk it from Sarah's place. But I've got to go out in an hour, so it had better be straight away – that means the noo. See you.' And without waiting for confirmation, he rang off.

'The noo indeed,' fumed Lisa, running a comb through her hair and hastily applying a rather basic make-up. If there was one thing she couldn't abide, it was a Sassenach trying to take off a Scots accent. She was not ashamed of the way she spoke, although she did not appreciate just how charming and subtle her accent was, the intonations north of the Grampians being a far cry from the guttural Glaswegian which typified the Scots way of speech to the more ignorant Southerner. Well, she reflected, she might have to meet all manner of toffee-nosed snobs in the course of her new profession, but if this Michael Delaney thought that he could get away with making a fool of her, he would soon have another think coming –

Lisa stopped herself, sighing. It was one thing getting the sack for insubordination; it was quite another, antagonising valuable clients. Now that she was self-employed, she would have to learn to govern that quick temper of hers. However insufferable Mr Delaney turned out to be, she must land this first all-important contract. Diplomacy must be her watchword.

12

As she was leaving, muttering good resolutions to herself, she suddenly remembered that today was early closing, and armed herself with her antique shopping trolley, which had belonged to her mother, before setting off for Montpelier Gardens. She defiantly took her time about getting there, calling in at the butcher's for a pound of liver, and at the greengrocer's for some onions. She had a recipe she wanted to try out on Sarah, who was supposed to be staying in that evening. Lisa was convinced that Sarah was anaemic. Liver was just what she needed to thicken up her blood.

Montpelier Gardens consisted of several blocks of imposing mansion flats. To gain access through the heavy glass doors, one was obliged to use an entryphone. Pressing the buzzer for number 28, Lisa was forced to announce herself into yet another infernal machine. There was a considerable delay before the sardonic voice, clipped and crackly, said lazily, 'Just walk in, Lisa, and wait. I'm in the middle of a phone call.'

The plate-glass doors clicked open. Lisa rejected the lift, fearing mishap, and walked up to the sixth floor, dragging her trolley behind her. The door of number 28 was already open.

The hall led directly into a starkly beautiful reception room, totally in monochrome − thick white carpet, black leather settees, glass and chrome tables, grey velvet curtains and plain white walls, adorned only with a series of large, glossy black-and-white photographs. Waiting as instructed, Lisa inspected these pictures, which she took at first to be abstracts. Only upon closer scrutiny did they reveal themselves as highly stylised, irreproachably tasteful nudes, fragmented, backlit, set against montages of ferns, branches, pebbles and rocks. The room was entirely free of other ornament or clutter.

Lisa could not somehow bring herself to sit down on a

13

luxurious settee, and after several minutes' wait she began to feel awkward just standing there with the nudes. A door off to the left was ajar, and guessing that this might be the kitchen, she peered inside.

Immaculate as a laboratory, resplendent in scarlet and dazzling white, and equipped with gleaming stainless steel fitments, it quite overawed her. Even the sink was polished to a mirror finish. How would she ever dare turn on a tap, let alone cook, in here? Practical by nature, Lisa was quite unused to the pristine, or the stylish. Her home in Auchterbrae was clean, but cosy, shabby even, and the flat she shared with Sarah was perennially untidy, littered as it was with Sarah's clothes, accessories and personal accoutrements, which seemed to invade every available corner of space.

Wandering, greatly impressed, back into the living-room, Lisa stopped in her tracks, gasping with horror. Oozing ominously through the wickerwork of her shopping trolley was a sinister pink liquid, which was dripping relentlessly into the thick, spotless pile of the expensive white carpet.

Moaning with terror, Lisa was galvanised into action. Rescuing the leaking parcel of liver, which had been protesting silently under the weight of the onions, she hurriedly seized an alabaster ashtray from a nearby coffee table, into which she deposited the sticky package. Running back into the kitchen, she rifled the drawers for a wiping-up cloth, eventually settling for a linen teatowel, being unable to find anything more humble. Wetting it hastily under the tap, she dashed back to the scene of the crime and began dabbing frantically at the stain, succeeding only in making it paler, but bigger. She was by now quite desperate to undo the damage before Michael Delaney appeared, and in her confusion, accidentally knocked over the offending trolley, sending onions

14

hurtling into every corner of the room, shedding debris as they rolled.

Nearly sobbing with panic, Lisa was compelled to abandon her efforts with the carpet to scrabble around on her hands and knees in hot pursuit, until, transfixed with horror, she found herself looking at a pair of feet, shod in dark blue trainers and attached to two very long denim-clad legs. An onion in each hand, Lisa looked up. Seen from her lowly position, Michael Delaney literally towered above her, arms folded and a look of wry astonishment on his face. For a moment nothing was said while they took each other in. Then, unpredictably, he squatted down beside her and picked up an onion, which he threw playfully up into the air and caught again, his eyes never leaving hers.

'Having oorselves a bonny wee Highland fling, are we?' he asked conversationally, giving a pretty good imitation of Billy Connolly.

Hapless in her guilt, Lisa did not dare react. He hadn't yet seen the stain on the carpet. Silently, she returned the straying onions to the shopping trolley and stubbornly resumed her dabbing with the soggy teatowel.

'Leave it,' barked Delaney in his normal voice, eyeing the contents of the ashtray. 'Someone comes in to clean. No need for a drama. Sit down, I don't bite.' He snatched the damp cloth from her and strode into the kitchen, bearing the liver at arm's length.

'Liver and onions, my mum used to do them a treat,' he remarked from the depths of the kitchen. 'Is that what you had in mind for Saturday's menu? Or were you planning an impromptu fry-up, to convince me of your talents? If I had more time, I'd take you up on that.'

Lisa sat down miserably, sinking inelegantly into the depths of a leather chair, craving invisibility. She was very seldom speechless. Her entire stock of impertinent remarks seemed to have deserted her. Just as well, she thought ruefully, she was in quite enough trouble already.

Delaney strolled back in and sprawled casually on one of the settees. The huge room seemed to diminish in size with his presence. He didn't speak straight away, surveying her provocatively with amused curiosity. Lisa stared back at him boldly. She would not, had she seen him in the street, have put him down for a photographer. His powerful build put her more in mind of the muscular farm workers back home. He was very dark, with jet black, curly hair, and his face had a tough and well-worn look, as if he habitually burned the candle at both ends, his sardonic expression indicating a vast and cynical experience of life. Physically, he emanated a sense of danger. But his eyes, undoubtedly, were the most wicked part of him. Twinkling with malevolence, they had evidently, at one time or another, seen it all. Except, perhaps, a red-haired woman on her hands and knees, chasing onions all over his flat.

When eventually he spoke, he went straight to the point.

'Saturday night, starting at about eight-thirty, I'm expecting twenty potential clients, plus partners. Pleasure from their point of view, business from mine. I'd like the catering to be unobtrusive — food they can help themselves to from that large table over there, and eat without getting it all over the walls. It doesn't need to be elaborate, they'll all be much more interested in the booze. I'll deal with that. I'd like you to stay until they've finished eating and keep the decks clear. I expect you charge by the hour, so you won't mind if it drags on a bit.'

He stood up and crossed to a black ash writing desk by the window, removed a chequebook and signed a cheque with a flourish. It was blank, apart from the signature.

16

'That's to take care of the food, I'll leave it all to you. I shall be here from about seven onwards, to let you in.'

Lisa couldn't believe it, especially after the recent débâcle. It was all so impossibly easy. She gazed at him dumbly, rooted to the spot. Unexpectedly, he dragged her to her feet, and propelled her towards the window, taking her head in both hands and swivelling it towards the light.

'Don't move,' he commanded, and walked backwards, never taking his eyes off her. 'Lift your head a little – look up!' Untypically, Lisa for once obeyed without demur, realising that she would be wise to appear co-operative by nature.

'Right,' he said abruptly, looking at his watch. 'I'm late for an appointment. I shall be wanting to take some pictures of you, but we'll talk about it another time. Meanwhile, don't mention it to Sarah, or she'll want to mess about with your hair and plaster your face with make-up.'

He opened the door wide. Wordlessly, Lisa reclaimed her shopping trolley and stepped outside into safety.

'Wait a minute,' he admonished, and disappeared briefly, returning with the alabaster ashtray.

'You nearly forgot your liver.'

He smiled unexpectedly, his face crinkling into an expression of conspiratorial mischief. She took it from him, blushing, as the gleaming white door closed behind her.

Chapter Two

After a great deal of careful thought, Lisa soon had her plans meticulously laid for her first venture into private catering. The weather being chilly for late April, she planned to start with piping hot savouries, followed by a large variety of bite-sized cold delicacies, all things that people could eat without juggling with knives and forks. She judged, correctly, that Michael Delaney would appreciate a menu which did not interfere with the conversation. To finish with, she baked tiny pastries, crammed with an apple and almond filling. These were her own invention, and quite delectable.

To compensate for the smallness of all these dainty morsels, she made vast quantities of everything. All the fiddly, tricky preparation was done during the day in the privacy of Sarah's flat, so that she would have only the final assembly and presentation to worry about on the night. This would give the illusion of effortless competence, which she was anxious to foster. She packed everything carefully in large cardboard boxes and rang, with panache, for a taxi. Turning on her best Celtic charm, she got the driver to load the boxes for her and unload them again at Montpelier Gardens. When he saw the size of the tip she gave him, he piled the boxes into the lift unbidden, and carried them into the kitchen of number 28 while Michael Delaney, damp from the shower and clad only in a bathrobe, looked on, bemused.

So far, so good, thought Lisa. She was determined to redeem herself after the fiasco of her first meeting with her client. She nodded good evening to him regally, and set to work without another word. Secretly, she had been a little worried that she might have exceeded the budget he had in mind, having got somewhat carried away in Harrods' Food Hall, but the sybaritic elegance of the flat reassured her that he clearly did not count the pennies when it came to matters of good taste.

Boldly, she started opening cupboards to see what he had in the way of dishes. She had brought a supply of paper plates, in case of emergency, but privately thought that they were not quite the thing. She need not have worried. He possessed stacks of unused-looking, plain white Rosenthal porcelain. She looked at her watch. Seven-thirty already. Deliberately, she had not arrived too early, reluctant to appear in any way over-anxious.

Lisa had not been at all sure what to wear for her first assignment, although Sarah had generously told her to borrow any of her clothes she fancied – a suggestion which was more well-meaning than practical, given Sarah's sylph-like measurements. In the end, Lisa had invested in a new Laura Ashley cotton print dress and a white, frilled, hostess apron, deciding that this would serve as a uniform for her catering forays – cool, comfortable, but sufficiently dressy not to make her seem dowdy amongst guests in their glad-rags. The outfit was in fact very becoming, set off jauntily by a white-frilled mob-cap – Lisa was punctilious about tying back her long hair when she was preparing food. All in all, she presented a very different picture from the panic-stricken creature with the shopping trolley whom Delaney had first encountered.

19

Disarmingly, he told her so. Strolling into the kitchen, he watched her at work for a few moments while she affected not to notice him, and then commented, 'Well, Lisa, I'm most impressed at the transformation. Anyone would think you'd done this kind of thing before.'

Lisa flushed. It didn't help, his knowing that this was her first engagement.

'I'd be grateful if you wouldn't enlighten any of your guests as to my lack of experience,' she replied dryly, adding cheekily, 'Like you, I'm hoping to drum up a bit of business this evening.'

'Your secret is safe with me,' he assured her, his eyes alight with devilment, helping himself to a smoked salmon wheel.

Why she did it, Lisa did not know, but, momentarily forgetting that this was her employer and the financier of the entire enterprise, she automatically smacked his hand away in the manner of a busy mother shooing away a meddlesome child. It was pure reflex, generated by suppressed nervousness.

'I'm sorry,' she corrected herself, retracting her hand as if she had burnt it. 'I forgot . . .' Crimson, she met his gaze. Unabashed, he helped himself to another one and fixed her with mocking black eyes, his face creased in amusement. Then he looked her slowly up and down, from her vivid green eyes down the length of her curvaceous figure, lingering insolently on her breasts. He seemed quite menacingly male, standing there evidently naked under the short bathrobe, every inch of exposed flesh covered in dark hair. Lisa had no experience of semiclothed men. Instinctively, she shrank from him, turning her back and busying herself to hide her confusion.

'Anything I can do to help?' he enquired smoothly.

'No thank you. Why don't you go and get yourself dressed instead?' she replied, before realising how bald

20

this sounded. She might as well have admitted outright that she found his déshabillé disturbing.

'As you wish,' he said gravely, behind her, and she started violently at the touch of his fingers on her neck. Surely he wasn't about to make a pass at her?

'Relax,' he taunted her. 'Some of your hair has come loose,' and he gently tucked it back under the elastic of the cap before leaving her to her labours.

Lisa had a natural flair for presentation, and soon the large glass table was draped in a snowy-white cloth and laden with plates of mouthwatering titbits, attractively garnished with greenstuff and artfully shaped decorations of radishes, tomatoes, lemon and cucumber. The lighting was subdued, the glassware glittering on the drinks trolley. The oven was preheating in readiness for the hot savouries a good half hour before the first guest was expected. So efficient had been her preparation that she found herself with nothing left to do, and paced the kitchen restlessly, unwilling to appear in the living-room at a loose end.

'Are you all right in there?' she heard Michael call, casually. 'Come and have a glass of wine. No need to skulk by the saucepans like a servant.'

'I'm busy,' she called back untruthfully.

'Liar,' he said, walking in, glass in hand, and viewing the immaculate order of the kitchen. He was less intimidating with his clothes on, looking effortlessly sartorial in a red open-necked shirt and white trousers. He held out the glass to her and walked back into the living-room, beckoning her coaxingly with a satirical index finger. She followed him, defeated.

His charm was insidious. As she sipped the cold white wine, he made innocent but well-aimed small talk which succeeded in drawing her out without revealing anything at all about himself. She might have been a guest herself

21

rather than a paid helper. Soon he knew all about her cookery course and her high-flown culinary ambitions. Lisa was naturally talkative, but despite her resolution to be cool, formal and dignified, she was no match for his manipulative skills. Of course, she thought wryly, he had to be good at relaxing people when he photographed them. Her eyes flew involuntarily to the nudes.

'I don't know how I came to be doing all the talking, I'm sure,' she found herself saying awkwardly, fiddling with her empty glass. 'I think I'll away back to the kitchen now. Your guests will be arriving any minute.'

'You're doing all the talking because I enjoy listening to you. You know, your accent is really quite irresistible. A sort of cross between the Prime of Miss Jean Brodie and Dr Finlay's Casebook.'

Lisa's eyes flashed. 'That's just about as ignorant as me saying that you sound like someone from Birmingham,' she retorted, aware, too late, that she must sound rude.

'You are a sensitive soul, aren't you, Lisa? Why are you on the defensive all the time? You must laugh sometimes or you wouldn't have those gorgeous dimples.'

Michael Delaney was obviously adept at shooting the appropriate line to any available woman. It was written all over him. Jet-setting photographer chats up country bumpkin, thought Lisa; no doubt he was thinking she looked a likely pushover. He set about outstaring her with those come-to-bed eyes. She shifted uncomfortably in her chair.

'It just gets very tedious, being teased about my accent,' she explained stiffly. 'It's a form of harassment, and it's irritating to think someone's listening to the way you speak rather than what you're saying. Now, if you think about it, your accent sounds just as odd to me, only I'm too polite to mention it.'

22

Unaccountably, he seemed to find this remark extraordinarily funny, laughing quietly to himself while Lisa looked at him blankly, until, suddenly serious, he said, in an unfamiliar, rasping, gravelly voice, 'The joke is this, love. *This* is the way I really speak, when I'm tired, or angry, or drinking with my old mates down Canning Town. So why should you be touchy? If I talked this way to the mob who are coming here tonight, they wouldn't take me seriously, see? Whereas you, dear Liza, sound so blooming genteel, they'll find your diction quite delightful.'

The words tumbled out of his mouth in the purest, most unadulterated Bow Bells Cockney, so unlike his usual classless, well-modulated tones as to render Lisa totally speechless.

'Surprised?' he grinned, reverting to his normal, cultivated voice. 'I got rid of my accent before it became fashionable to keep it. Pity, really, because dampened down Cockney's all the rage these days among trendy photographers. When I first started trying to sell pictures, I was working on a building site in Poplar. I didn't trust my work enough to let it speak for me, so I ditched my accent along with a lot of other things about myself. Quite a cop-out, I suppose, I'm not particularly proud of it, but talking like this comes naturally now. So don't ever think I'd presume to make fun of your accent – or anyone else's, for that matter.'

The entryphone buzzed. Lisa dived into the kitchen. The party had begun.

She was gratified at the inroads Michael's guests made into the food she had prepared. It disappeared as fast as she could replenish it. The company was glittering, the women glamorously dressed and reeking of expensive perfume. Lisa was glad of her new outfit as she darted unobtrusively in and out of the living-room. Apart from a

23

brilliant smile from Sarah and a knowing wink from Richard, she was relieved to be politely ignored, except by Michael, that is, who looked in on her once or twice to ask if everything was okay.

'They're gobbling the food as if there were no tomorrow,' he informed her dryly. 'Given the flesh-pots this lot are used to, I think you can take that as a compliment.'

Standing just inside the doorway of the kitchen, Lisa was able to view the progress of the party unobserved. The guests had appeased their initial hunger, and there was enough on the buffet table now to keep them going until she decided it was time to bring on the sweet pastries.

The women at the party filled her with envy. Sarah was, of course, an absolute knock-out in turquoise silk, but she was, after all, a model. The other women were simply wives and girlfriends of picture editors, PR executives and the like, rather than professional fashion plates, but they all seemed to have that cool, sophisticated elegance which Lisa so much admired. In her opinion, the best-looking woman there was undoubtedly a tall, graceful blonde, very, very slim with a wonderfully regal posture. She was dressed in a simple, low-cut, close fitting, white dress, which emphasised her expensive tan, as did the numerous heavy gold chains which adorned her neck. Lisa couldn't help noticing the sultry looks she kept flinging in Michael's direction, not that he appeared to acknowledge these. Whoever the proud Davina was, the girlfriend who had recently walked out on him, he had evidently not yet got round to replacing her.

Sarah, briefly visiting Lisa in the kitchen to tell her how well she was doing, explained briefly that the striking blonde was Barbara Bentley, the wife of Howard Bentley, the prospective publisher of Michael's new book, but as usual her narrative digressed as to where Barbara bought her clothes and how wonderfully thin she

24

was, and before long she had drifted back into the throng.

Lisa sat down on the workbench and made herself a quiet cup of tea. There would be little for her to do for the next hour or so. Nosily, she looked in the fridge and the cupboards. She could only assume that Michael Delaney always ate out, as apart from numerous packs of ground coffee, a few anonymous tea bags, and a packet of cream crackers, he did not seem to keep any provisions in stock. The enormous fridge was full of bottles of Perrier water, cartons of orange juice, and cans of German lager. A large black plastic bag in the salad bin turned out to contain innumerable rolls of film, and the freezer compartment was empty apart from one rather forlorn loaf of bread. All that money and success, she thought, and the poor man never had the taste of good home cooking. Maybe he hadn't been joking about testing out the liver and onions.

Lisa fell into one of the typically convoluted day-dreams which had so seriously blighted her office career. She pictured herself as the doyenne of a top-flight cater-ing establishment, employing a team of qualified cooks to visit the kitchens of the rich and famous – herself, Lisa Campbell, retaining a generous override commission on their services and imposing a hefty surcharge on the food which she would, naturally, obtain at skilfully negotiated wholesale prices. Following that, she might mastermind an exclusive gourmet restaurant, and perhaps eventually set up her own cookery school. Exotic dishes would be named after her, and she would write the definitive cookery book which would outsell Mrs Beeton.

This reverie had quite taken hold of her when she was brought back to earth by the sound of a shrill female voice protesting loudly and incoherently. Whoever was speaking sounded on the brink of hysteria. Before she could peer into the next room to see the cause of the

25

commotion, Michael put his head round the door and rapped out, 'Coffee, Lisa, black and strong, and quick,' and disappeared again, closing the door. Lisa switched on the filter coffee machine, which was already loaded, and pulled the door ajar so that she could see through the gap.

Michael and Howard Bentley seemed to be trying to persuade Barbara Bentley into the bedroom next door. She was objecting noisily, elbows flailing. She was complaining angrily about someone called James not loving her any more, the blame for this devolving, it appeared, on to either Michael, or Howard, or both of them. Michael wore a look of badly concealed exasperation, while Howard, a genial but rather helpless-looking man in his late forties, was clearly horribly embarrassed.

Lisa realised that fast action was required. A small amount of coffee had by now dripped into the jug. She poured it quickly into a china cup and slid into the next room. Silently, she crossed to the scene of the fracas, and handed the cup to Michael. Everyone else was affecting not to have noticed Barbara's outburst, although their polite dissimulation grew more uneasy by the minute.

'Sit down, Babs,' said Michael, with a steely quietness. 'Drink this and then Howard will take you home. You're overtired.'

'Dying to get rid of me, aren't you?' spat Barbara, her upper class vowels cutting through the air like a rapier. 'I don't want any bloody coffee. I want another gin.'

Suddenly, the cup was knocked sideways by her impatient gesture, and the boiling hot coffee flooded all over her bare arm. Predictably, she shrieked with pain.

Catching a look of despair on Michael's face, Lisa, to her amazement, took charge.

'Come with me,' she found herself saying to Barbara, gently but firmly taking her undamaged arm. The cool,

26

melodic, unfamiliar voice miraculously captured Barbara's attention. Like a weeping child, who has been suddenly distracted, her tantrum abated under Lisa's calm gaze. Instinctively sensing sympathy, she softened, and, while an astonished Michael and Howard looked on, allowed herself, docile as a lamb, to be led down the hallway and into the luxurious bathroom, where Lisa sat her down on a wicker chair and locked them both in.

Opening the medicine cabinet, she found some suitable ointment and a lint bandage, and set about dressing the scald.

'What a shame about your lovely white dress,' soothed Lisa. 'I'll try to get those stains out for you in just a minute.'

'I don't know you,' stated Barbara, petulantly. 'You don't look like one of Michael's floozies.'

'I'm not a guest,' responded Lisa impassively, snipping a length of bandage. 'I'm the cook. Mr Delaney hired me for the evening.'

Barbara whimpered rather excessively as Lisa gently bandaged her arm, tactfully ignoring her frequent un-ladylike expletives. She hoped to keep Barbara talking until she'd calmed down and sobered up a bit. As it happened, Barbara needed no prompting to unleash a verbal torrent on her captive audience.

'I see he's got rid of that bitch Davina,' she muttered, as Lisa dabbed at the coffee stains. 'I never knew what he saw in her, except that she was easy meat. Did you notice him eyeing that girl in the turquoise dress? She was giving him the green light, all right.'

Lisa didn't know whether to be appalled or amused. Did this woman have an unrequited passion for Michael, was she a jealous old flame, or what?

'The beastly party's a great success, don't you think? The bastard always gets everybody eating out of his hand.

27

Look at the advance he's wangled out of Howard on his rotten book. High class pornography, if you ask me. You've got to hand it to Michael, he knows how to make a fast buck. I'm thirsty,' she announced, looking purposefully towards the door.

'Wait a minute,' forestalled Lisa firmly. 'I haven't finished with your dress yet.'

'I wouldn't mind, if it wasn't for James,' continued Barbara broodingly. 'I draw the line at him poisoning his mind against me.'

And who was this James? puzzled Lisa silently to herself. Some prospective paramour? Was Michael trying to put a spoke in some extra-marital affair? If so, why? To protect Howard? She kept sponging away at the dress, and wondered vaguely if Michael Delaney possessed such a humble object as an iron. If she could get Barbara to take the dress off while she pressed it, she would be obliged to withdraw from the party for as long as it took, by which time, hopefully, the more vituperative effects of the gin would have worn off. She was just pondering the mechanics of this brainwave when she registered that Barbara's mutterings had temporarily ceased. Sprawled out inelegantly in the wicker armchair, she had fallen fast asleep.

Lisa crept out of the bathroom. Michael, who was giving an excellent impersonation of a man without a care in the world, caught her eye as soon as she re-entered the room, and excused himself urbanely from the group he was chatting with. As if by unspoken arrangement, he followed her into the kitchen and shut the door.

'I dressed her arm and now she's dozed off,' explained Lisa succinctly, piling sweet pastries on to a plate. Michael looked relieved, and then, unpredictably, amused.

'How many badges?' he asked.

'What?' queried Lisa, thinking she had misheard him.

'When you were a girl guide. Hostess badge, first aid badge, how many others? What were you like at tying knots?'

'Will you kindly get out of my road, please?' responded Lisa primly, preparing to sail past him with a loaded dish. He took it from her and put it down.

'Thank you, Lisa,' he said softly, taking her in his arms and kissing the top of her head. 'You're a braw wee lassie.' He held her briefly, then released her abruptly, and left her to return to his guests. Lisa leaned back against the workbench, finding that, for some reason, she had suddenly gone weak at the knees.

When she next entered the room to serve the dessert and set out the coffee cups, she noticed that Howard Bentley had gone, presumably to take his wife home. Everyone carried on as if the incident had never happened. From then on she was kept busy serving coffee and clearing away the empty plates. The kitchen had reverted to its habitual untouched appearance, and Lisa was dropping with weariness, by the time Sarah and Richard announced their departure and offered her a lift home. Gratefully, she accepted, and managed to leave without bidding Michael Delaney goodbye.

Exhausted, she dozed off in the back of the car, and went straight to bed when they got home, not wishing to play gooseberry to Richard's amorous lingerings. The evening, she reflected, must have taxed her more than she had realised. She slept heavily and rose untypically late, to find Sarah already picking at her breakfast over the Sunday papers.

'Super food, darling,' Sarah greeted her. 'People were frightfully impressed. They'll all be ringing Michael up wanting your phone number, you'll see. Those anchovy whatnots were sublime.'

29

'Thanks,' acknowledged Lisa, sleepily filling the kettle. 'The party seemed to go quite well, I thought.'

'All things considered. I call it bad management on Michael's part, though, having Howard as his publisher. It's bound to make things ultra-complicated. Richard and I were talking about it after you went to bed.'

'He seemed a nice man – Howard, I mean,' mused Lisa, not quite getting Sarah's drift, 'although he looked a bit henpecked to me.'

Sarah chortled gaily. 'That's the understatement of the year. Barbara leads the poor fellow a dog's life, and of course everybody knows she's got the most spectacular drink problem. Richard says she never really got over Michael.'

'Oh, I see,' nodded Lisa, enlightened. 'I suspected from what she said that they might have had an affair or something.'

'An affair? Oh, nothing as simple as that. For his sins, the poor chap was actually married to her. Can you imagine?' Clearly, Sarah found the idea of this marriage vastly entertaining.

Lisa let out a deep sigh as the penny finally dropped.

'I can't really, no,' she agreed, after a moment. 'I wouldn't have thought he'd be likely to get involved with someone so . . . sensitive.'

'Oh, you are sweet, Lisa. Never like to say an unkind word, do you? Not like me. I adore scandal. Let me fill you in.'

When she made the effort to shed her customary vagueness, Sarah was an enthusiastic raconteur. While Lisa sipped her tea, wide-eyed, she passed on, with a flourish, some more of the inside information she had evidently pumped out of Richard.

Michael, as Lisa already knew, had come from humble origins in the East End, and had started off his working

30

life as a bricklayer. (That must be how he got those muscles, thought Lisa). He had always had a passion for photography, and, thwarted in his attempts to turn professional conventionally, he had quite suddenly ditched the building trade and 'dropped out', travelling overland to Australia in search of saleable subject matter and untapped markets. On reaching Hong Kong, he had made the necessary U.S. military contacts to get himself into Viet Nam, and at the potential cost of his life had made a rapid name for himself as a committed and apparently fearless war photographer, powerfully capturing the misery and horror of what he saw in dramatic and disturbing pictures.

Soon after returning to London, he had met and married Barbara, the daughter of a well-connected property millionaire. According to Sarah, Barbara had been swept off her feet by Michael's direct, unsophisticated working-class charm. ('Hardly the type of man she was used to.') The union had been a brief and stormy one, and a lot of mud had been thrown around as to what had gone wrong. Barbara had remarried soon after the divorce, and Michael, having made his name, had retired from war photography and now picked and chose his assignments. He'd recently produced a controversial feature on slum housing for one of the Sunday colour supplements, and was currently putting together a book on women.

'Other photographers have done it before, of course, but this one is expected to be sensational,' explained Sarah wistfully. 'Models and actresses are falling over themselves to get into it, but by all accounts he's being hyper-selective. No one knows exactly what he's got in mind, not even Howard. But whatever's in it, it's bound to sell. His stuff's terribly in vogue at the moment.'

These revelations gave Lisa considerable food for

thought. She was certainly seeing a side to life which had, until now, been quite outside her experience. She didn't know what to make of Michael Delaney himself, the central character in this unfamiliar scenario. He was, she judged, a bit of a womaniser, and big-headed with it. Clearly he must have hurt the unfortunate Barbara very badly indeed for the poor woman to have hit the bottle like that, especially when she had so much going for her – still beautiful, evidently wealthy, and remarried to a successful publisher, who seemed, from Lisa's first impression of him, to be a kind and considerate husband. Although, she had to admit, Howard Bentley must be a bit of a contrast after Michael Delaney. Balding, slightly paunchy, bespectacled and bemused, he had none of Michael's smouldering masculinity.

'Poor old Barbara,' continued Sarah, her eyes slightly dreamy. 'She was a fool to give him up, if you ask me. I could put up with an awful lot from a man like that. What did you think of him?'

Lisa buried her face in her teacup, aware that it had flooded with colour as she suddenly remembered that odd, unheralded embrace in the kitchen.

'There's nothing worse, in my opinion,' she declared primly, 'than a man who fancies himself.'

Sarah grinned knowingly.

'What you mean is, *you* fancied him!'

'I most certainly did not,' protested Lisa hotly, turning her back on Sarah and attacking the washing-up with gusto. 'I was there in a professional capacity. Mr Delaney is my client. It was strictly business, and it would be very poor practice for me to start fancying the people who hire me. Naturally, I hope he'll be engaging me again. Would you have any idea, Sarah, what I ought to charge him for last night? I supose I should send him a bill through the post.'

32

'Oh, charge him a bomb, darling. He can afford it. People never value what they get cheap. Just think what it would have cost him to take us all to a restaurant.'

Lisa was shocked. 'I wouldn't dream of overcharging him,' she protested, shaking her head. 'Apart from anything else, he doesn't strike me as the type of man who'd allow himself to be rooked.'

'You really are an innocent abroad, Lisa. Would you like me to tell you the fee he can charge for just one day of his time? More than I earn in a month, I can assure you. This is the big city. You want to get tuned in.' Sarah's expression became pensive again. 'If Michael Delaney made a play for *me*,' she mused, reverting to her previous theme, 'I'd ditch Richard like a shot. I thought I caught him giving me the once-over – you didn't happen to clock it, did you?'

'No, I didn't, but his ex-wife did,' Lisa informed her dryly. 'She noticed him eyeing you. But, I must say, she does seem to be a very jealous lady, and she was rather drunk into the bargain. She even asked me if *I* was one of his floozies! And she wasn't very complimentary about that Christina.'

'Davina,' Sarah corrected her. 'She appears to have made the cardinal error. Richard heard on the grapevine that she was starting to hallucinate about the old wedding bells. Silly girl! Michael's had enough of marriage, by all accounts. Can you blame him? No, any girl who wants Michael takes him on his terms or not at all. He's a very hard man, very tough – which can be terribly sexy, don't you think?'

Lisa sighed. Sarah's prattling was becoming tiresome.

'I really wouldn't know, Sarah. I'm just not interested in men right now.'

'Don't be so straitlaced, darling,' smirked Sarah. 'You want to loosen up a bit or you'll never have any

33

fun. Plus, if you don't mind my saying so, you do tend to come over as green as grass. If you don't get wised up, sooner or later some rotten swine will eat you for breakfast.'

'When I need your advice, Sarah,' Lisa informed her friend coldly, 'I'll not hesitate to ask you for it.'

'Any time, darling,' teased Sarah, as Lisa marched off to get dressed.

That evening, Lisa, alone in the flat, settled down to enjoy a long, luxurious bath, helping herself liberally to one of Sarah's numerous foaming preparations. She had washed her hair, and was wallowing contentedly in the fragrant water with a particularly gripping and bloodthirsty thriller. She had just got to the third murder, and was leaning forward to run in some more hot, when the phone started to ring. She resolved to ignore it. Phone calls were always for Sarah, and Lisa was heartily sick of acting as social secretary and message taker. On the tenth ring, however, it occurred to her with a jolt that this could be one of Michael Delaney's guests phoning up to enlist her services.

She leapt belatedly out of the bath, grabbing a towel, and careered, dripping, into the hall. Those answering machines had something to be said for them after all, she thought, seizing the receiver.

'Lisa Campbell speaking,' she gasped.

'Good evening,' drawled a cultured, faintly familiar voice. 'This is Barbara Bentley. I daresay you remember me from last night.' There was just a hint of dry, unapologetic irony in her tone.

'Oh, good evening, Mrs Bentley,' replied Lisa, slightly flustered. Barbara Bentley was the last person she would have expected to hear from. 'How's your arm?'

'It hurts like hell,' Barbara informed her crisply.

34

'This cookery thing you do ... I've just sacked the housekeeper and the au pair can't boil an egg. I want you to come and fix Sunday lunch for eight next weekend. Can you do it?' She sounded bored, impatient, and extremely sober.

'I'll just check my diary,' responded Lisa, purposefully rustling the pad by the telephone. 'Yes, that's lucky. I've just had a cancellation.'

'Good. We're going to be at our cottage in Lynford Bassett − that's in the New Forest. If you take the ten-fifteen from Waterloo, my husband will meet you at Southampton station. Don't worry about bringing any food. I get it all delivered. All right?'

'Yes, that'll be fine,' confirmed Lisa, as Barbara hung up abruptly. Another booking already! The world was surely going to be her oyster. She quickly wrote down '10.15 Sunday, Waterloo − Lynford Bassett' and skipped gleefully back into the bathroom, throwing aside the towel and plopping back into the warm water. She retrieved her rather damp paperback and re-immersed herself in the convolutions of the plot.

Five minutes later the phone rang again. She did not hesitate this time. Another client! She really would need to buy herself a diary at this rate. She quickly trod the same soggy trail across the carpet and picked up the phone again.

'Lisa Campbell speaking,' she informed the caller eagerly.

''Allo?' enquired a coarse, gritty voice. 'Miss Campbell? This is the Bricklayer's Arms, Wapping. Mick Delaney gave us your name. We've got a big do coming up Friday night, and the cook's run off with the barman. Can you 'elp us out?'

Lisa was flabbergasted. The Bricklayer's Arms, Wapping? Where on earth was that?

35

'Er . . . I'm not sure,' she wavered uncertainly. She was hardly in a position to turn work down, but this did not sound at all the kind of engagement she had in mind. 'Perhaps I should point out right away,' she hedged boldly, 'that I do tend to specialise, and I am very expensive.'

A raucous, rather filthy laugh greeted this pronouncement. 'No problem, luv. Friday's pay day, like. We can always get the lads to have a bit of a whip-round.'

'And what exactly would you be wanting me to cook?' demanded Lisa guardedly. The landlord of the Bricklayer's Arms sounded very much the beery, uncouth, slap-and-tickle type, more in need of a buxom serving wench than a cordon-bleu cook. This was indeed a far cry from lunch for eight at Lynford Bassett.

'Oh, you know the type of thing, ducks. Jellied eels, pie and mash, boiled beef and carrots, liver and onions . . .' The voice began to shake with barely suppressed laughter. There was an ominous pause while Lisa took a deep breath.

'I don't happen to think that was very funny,' she told Michael Delaney with some asperity. 'I got out of a nice hot bath to answer this call.'

'Did you indeed?' asked Michael, reverting to his habitual soft, suggestive sexy voice. 'Like me to come over and scrub your back for you?'

'I'll be sending you a bill in the post,' Lisa informed him crossly, hurriedly changing the subject.

'Perhaps I should start looking for a mortgage. You didn't bother to warn *me* you were very expensive. Just how much are you planning to hit me for?'

Lisa hesitated, reluctant to pluck the still undecided figure out of the air.

'As I said,' she prevaricated, 'I will be sending you a bill. Payment within fourteen days, if you don't mind.'

'That'll teach me to do business with a Scot,' he observed, infuriatingly. 'Dry yourself quickly, if you must. I'm coming over with the money right away.' And he hung up.

Fuming and pink from her bath, Lisa flung on jeans and a sweater and frantically set about drying her hair, not a quick task at the best of times, it being long, abundant and thick. She really ought to get it cut short, she thought, tugging at it irritably, and tint it a nice dark chestnut. Sarah, in a kind moment, had once described it as Titian. As far as Lisa was concerned, however, it was just plain old Campbell red.

The doorbell rang, long and loud. Sighing, Lisa tied back her damp tresses in a pony tail, and went to open the door with studied coolness. Her nonchalance evaporated at the sight of Michael standing there, large, dark and dangerous. He didn't make any move to come in.

'Hurry up,' he admonished. 'You'll need a coat, it's chilly and your hair's still wet.'

'A coat? But I'm not going anywhere!'

'Of course you are. You're coming back to my flat. I keep all my money under the mattress. And besides, I told you I wanted to take some pictures of you, remember?'

'Don't be ridiculous,' retorted Lisa. 'My hair's a mess and I haven't put on any make-up.'

'That's what I figured. It'll save you having to wash it all off. And I wanted your hair kind of . . . primitive.'

Seeing Lisa's well-worn mac hanging on a peg in the hall, he stepped inside, seized it, flung it round her shoulders, and hustled her out on to the landing.

There simply wasn't time to protest. A taxi was already waiting outside, and without another word he bundled her into it.

Chapter Three

'I'm cooking Sunday lunch for Mrs Bentley next weekend,' blurted out Lisa in the cab, feeling a need to break out of her initial speechlessness.

'I know,' said Michael lazily. 'Howard rang me earlier to ask for your phone number. I'm glad,' he added blandly. 'Babs could do with some decent grub inside her. Mind you, do plenty of roast potatoes. James has a passion for eating them cold.'

Lisa could contain her curiosity about the mysterious James no longer.

'Who exactly is James?' she asked brazenly.

'My son. He's seven. Now there's someone with a healthy appetite. He adores chips. He can put away any amount of them. Barbara only does those oven chips. Don't ever try to fob him off with those, he doesn't rate them.'

She should have guessed, of course. James was the product of the unfortunate marriage, the child whom Barbara claimed Michael had turned against her. Young James, thought Lisa, must be a perfect monster if he took after either or both of his parents. Poor kid, what chance did he have? Plainly Michael assumed that Lisa knew of his relationship with Barbara. No doubt he guessed Sarah had filled her in.

38

Montpelier Gardens was only a few minutes away by taxi. It had one of those rather intimidating old-fashioned lifts with a concertina-type door. There was only just room for two of them in it, and it creaked its way upwards with splendid sedateness. Once inside, Lisa stared at her feet while Michael scrutinised her openly. Eventually the lift shuddered to a halt and Michael strode briskly into the flat, leaving Lisa to follow at a distance. He disappeared into a room at the far end of the hall.

'I want some studio shots of you today in black and white,' he told her as she joined him. 'Then, another time, I might take some colour stuff out of doors. Something wistful on a hillside or in a field of buttercups. Sounds corny, but it won't look it, I promise you.'

The room was huge, high-ceilinged, and full of photographic paraphernalia. There were lights and reflectors everywhere, and a Hasselblad stood menacingly on a tripod in the centre of the studio.

'Perhaps you'd nip into the bedroom — the one off the living-room — and slip off your things,' he said casually, fiddling with the lights. 'Then we can have some coffee while the strap marks fade. I would have told you on the phone not to put on a bra, but I knew you'd probably barricade yourself in and dial 999. There's a dressing-gown hanging up on the door.'

There was a heavy silence.

'I suppose,' observed Lisa, with dignity, 'that this is another of your jokes. You're welcome to photograph my face, if you must, but that, I'm afraid, is all. In the circumstances, will you still be wanting that coffee?'

'Might as well. I can always spike yours with vodka on the quiet. I expect you're immune to whisky.'

'I think you're very rude,' Lisa informed him frostily. She had half a mind to leave on the spot, but told herself that now she was here, she would hold him to his promise to pay her for last night.

He blithely ignored this acid remark, absorbed in his equipment and, for lack of anything else to do, she stalked off to make the coffee as bidden, with much unnecessary clattering of crockery. He didn't reappear for some minutes, by which time she was sitting stiffly on one of the settees, with two cups steaming on a glass table. She glared at him.

'No milk or sugar, thanks,' he said amiably, settling himself down opposite her. He was dressed, unpretentiously, in old working clothes – faded but well-fitting jeans and a short-sleeved teeshirt, revealing strong, hairy, powerful-looking arms. All that hod-carrying, she reflected dryly. Pity he hadn't stuck to his former honest trade rather than inveigling unsuspecting women to strip off in front of his camera.

'You wouldn't be a Minister's daughter, by any chance?' he asked unexpectedly, with feigned seriousness. 'You have a fine upstanding air of the kirk about you.'

'My father,' responded Lisa icily, 'is a doctor. Not that it's any business of yours.'

'A doctor? All the more surprising, then, that you should be prudish about the human body. I suppose your father's patients do take their clothes off as necessary when he examines them?'

'That is *quite* a different matter,' fulminated Lisa. 'You cannot possibly be comparing yourself to a doctor!'

'Well, I admit I get to pick and choose my victims, but the point I'm making is that the photographic process is entirely asexual. I would never dream of taking advantage of a model, any more than your father would a patient. Quite apart from that, everything I do is considered to be in the most impeccable taste. Would you like to see some examples?'

'No thank you very much,' bit back Lisa, desperately trying to ignore the nudes on the wall. 'If we can just settle up for last night, I think I'll be on my way.'

'If you like,' continued Michael, reasonably, choosing to ignore her digression, 'I could take my clothes off as well. Would that make you feel more comfortable? I'd be happy to oblige.'

Lisa knew that he was baiting her now, and cursed herself for blushing, so predictably, at this remark. He was deliberately mocking her lack of sophistication, knowing that it rankled to be thought a prude, a small-town virgin with a phobia about nudity. She sat silent, glowering into her coffee cup. Michael vanished back into the studio and returned with a large portfolio under one arm. He settled himself down next to her on the settee.

'I'm working on a book,' he explained patiently. 'The idea is to capture the essence of femininity, from infancy through to old age. Howard has agreed to publish it some time next year. I told him I wasn't prepared to rush it. This is the preliminary material, the pictures I've selected so far. I haven't shown it to anyone before — you don't have to believe that but it happens to be true. Have a look through it. I think it proves my good faith. I'll leave you to it for a while. I've got things to do next door.' He put the folio on the table and left her.

Reluctantly, Lisa picked it up and started turning over the pages. She was no expert on photography, but, even to her untutored eye, the pictures were extraordinary. They were not, as she had assumed, mostly nudes — very few were, in fact. There were charming, witty portraits of little girls and some haunting shots of old women. Plus innumerable studies of strikingly beautiful women, some

41

of them famous, all of them characterised by the candid, unposed quality of their expressions. The overriding effect was that all Michael's subjects had either completely forgotten, or been unaware of, his camera.

Lisa looked at the photographs long and hard, feeling strangely humbled seeing them in the context of what Sarah had told her that morning. Michael Delaney had been committed enough to his craft to risk being killed for it in someone else's war. He had dragged himself up from obscurity by sheer talent, persistence and guts. How narrow-minded, hostile and priggish she would seem, refusing to accept a coveted place in a prestige volume like this. Sarah would have been beside herself at the thought of featuring in this book. And in any case, Michael Delaney had no doubt seen any number of women without their clothes. Right enough, he probably viewed them as clinically as a doctor.

Plainly, he wasn't about to plead with her. If she refused, he would shrug her off as a hicksville puritan and find himself some more amenable subject matter. After all, models and actresses were purportedly falling over themselves to sit for him. Why me? wondered Lisa, with sudden astonishment. When he could ask any woman he liked, why on earth does he want me?

Deep in thought, she didn't notice him return. Disconcerted, she realised that he had been observing her for some time.

'Why exactly do you want to take a picture of me?' she asked him guilelessly. He crouched down in front of her and looked levelly into her eyes.

'Because there's something ... unique about you. I noticed it the first time I saw you.'

Lisa would rather he hadn't referred to the first time he had seen her.

'What exactly?' she pursued, stubbornly, meeting his gaze steadily.

He hesitated. 'Don't take this the wrong way. You have the most wonderfully pure, innocent, virginal face on a very womanly, highly erotic body. The combination is quite startling. Now you're going to go all embarrassed on me.'

'I'm not embarrassed,' insisted Lisa, blushing crimson.

'You represent something very fleeting, very rare, that I've been looking for and haven't been able to find. Virgins with your sex appeal don't stay virgins for long, you see, and then the eyes change and the quality I'm trying to capture is lost. Are there many like you in Auchterbrae? There certainly aren't in London.'

Lisa wasn't sure whether she felt flattered or humiliated at this frank, and accurate, assumption of her virginity. But for once his eyes were serious, penetratingly so, and he was not making fun of her. In a sudden, strange, instinctive sort of way, she found herself able to trust him.

'I've never liked having my photo taken,' Lisa felt bound to confess. The pictures in the Campbell family album usually featured Lisa with her eyes shut or the top of her head chopped off. 'All the women in the book seem, well, relaxed — as if they don't know you're there. I'm afraid I'd look very stiff and awkward, I couldn't help it, 'specially without any clothes on . . .' Aware that she sounded more gauche by the minute, she finished firmly, 'The point is, I really think you'd be wasting your time.'

He smiled. 'If you were to look stiff and awkward, Lisa, it would be entirely my fault and not yours. Have you heard of Henri Cartier-Bresson?'

Lisa shook her head, feeling miserably ignorant.

'He's a famous French photographer, quite simply the best there is. He coined a phrase to describe precisely when you must press the shutter. A split second either way and you've blown it. He called it, "the decisive moment". It's up to me to seize the decisive moment that encapsulates what I want to say about you. You don't have to do anything at all. It's quite different from what Sarah does when Richard's taking fashion shots. Without her skill as a model, Richard would be in difficulty, because he's taking the clothes and Sarah has to give them life. You're very much alive already. All you have to do is let me look at you.'

Lisa gulped, fiddling nervously with her coffee spoon.

'Besides,' he continued, 'I can't do anything with the pictures unless you sign a release form. Otherwise you could sue me if I published them. That's the law when a picture is posed for in private, rather than taken in a public place — the street, for example. Usually I get a model to sign the release form before we start. Celebrities, especially, can get temperamental if the shot doesn't flatter them, and I refuse to waste time or film on their egos. But, in your case, you needn't sign the form until you've vetted the pictures. And if you have the slightest doubt about any of them, or you wish afterwards that you hadn't let me take them, then you needn't sign, and you can tear up the prints and destroy the negatives. Those aren't my usual terms, I might add. I happen to want these pictures very badly. In fact, I've never had to beg anyone to sit for me before. My fatal charm must be on the wane.'

Lisa looked at him for a long, hard moment. He met her gaze unwaveringly.

'In that case,' she said carefully, uncomfortably aware of the sound of her own voice, 'I'm prepared to give it a try.'

He didn't take her up on it immediately.

'Quite sure now? I promise not to sulk.'

'If I say I'll do it, I mean I'll do it,' stated Lisa firmly, hiding her nerves with a display of brisk impatience. 'But I haven't got all night. Where did you say I was to change?'

The studio was very warm; he must have turned the heating up, she thought. Nevertheless, Lisa was shivering under the bathrobe, the same one Michael had been wearing the night of the party. It smelt disturbingly of his aftershave. She was acutely conscious of the intimacy of having it next to her own bare skin.

He had seated her on a comfortable chaise-longue. The photoflood lights were as bright as day. They had made her squint at first, but her eyes were gradually getting used to them. There was, despite her trepidation, an unexpected air of normality about the whole operation, which had seemed prospectively so nerve-racking.

Michael chatted easily to her as he peered through the viewfinder and adjusted the lighting. Unhurried and relaxed, he questioned her casually about her cookery with apparently genuine interest. For someone who spent no time at all in the kitchen, he was surprisingly well informed about food. He had travelled extensively in the course of his work, and had eaten some very strange dishes indeed, especially in the Far East.

'Singapore sounds very exotic,' remarked Lisa, more at ease now. 'Would you believe, I've never been abroad at all? Sarah told me, of course, that you were in Viet Nam.'

'That's right,' he confirmed shortly, clearly disinclined to pursue this particular topic.

'I never really understood what the war was all about,' continued Lisa, undeterred by his reticence. 'I was only a

45

child at the time. It must have been quite horrible, seeing it all first-hand.'

'That's as good a word as any,' he said, firmly closing the subject. 'Let's just say I prefer what I'm doing now. Can you dispose of the pony-tail, please?'

Chastened, she shook her hair loose, thankful, as the fiery mane descended, that he was using monochrome.

He spent about twenty minutes taking the pictures. He took the robe from her unceremoniously and hung it up, and then positioned her accurately, his hands warm and impersonal on her face and shoulders. He was so coolly professional, so meticulous, so politely appreciative, that miraculously she felt neither self-conscious nor embarrassed. He gave her a layman's commentary on what he was doing with the equipment, which she found fascinating and distracting. She ceased to notice the rhythmic whirr of the motor drive or the glare of the artificial lights. She felt uncharacteristically compliant, a strange sense of languor enveloping her. It seemed to take no time at all; it was over before she knew it. Gently, he draped the robe back over her shoulders and said, 'Thank you, Lisa. That went extremely well.'

Quietly dressing again in his bedroom, she felt a certain anti-climax, as the intoxication of the experience began to wear off. She looked furtively around the room, deeply curious. The décor was starkly masculine, in sombre browns. As in the living-room, there was no clutter whatsoever. There was just one framed photograph on the wall, of a little boy scowling belligerently at the camera. There was no mistaking the mop of curly black hair or the tough line of the jaw. A miniature replica of his father, and obviously a child to be reckoned with, it was undoubtedly James Delaney.

Lisa was not disposed to linger, feeling illogically more

46

awkward after the session than she had done before. Michael called her a taxi.

'Don't forget the money I owe you,' he reminded her, as he helped her into her coat. 'How much did you say it was?'

'Well,' mumbled Lisa, noticing a mischievous glint in his eye, 'I was thinking in terms of £5 an hour, £25 in all.' He looked surprised. She felt somewhat abashed, afraid that he must think her mercenary.

'Don't be ridiculous,' barked Michael, calmly counting out ten-pound notes. 'You're not charging for all the time you spent preparing the stuff at home.' And he thrust £50 into her hand with a look that brooked no argument.

'Don't undersell yourself,' he lectured her sternly, ''specially if you're going to be cooking for Barbara. She spends more than that every time she goes to the hairdresser.'

He went down in the lift with her.

'I'll call you when the prints are ready,' he said, shutting the cab door. He gave her address to the driver, handed him the fare, raised his hand in a farewell salute, and disappeared through the doorway.

Lisa went straight to bed on arriving back at the flat, afraid somehow to be still up and about when Sarah arrived home. She felt that she would not be able to look her friend in the eye. Lying there in the dark, delayed-action shame washed over her in hot waves. No man had ever seen her naked. Lisa had always accepted the tenets of her sheltered upbringing without question. Certain privileges were reserved for husbands, and husbands alone. There was no permissive society in Auchterbrae.

Of course, Michael hadn't coerced her, hadn't used deceit or stealth, relying solely on his subtle, imperceptible, undoubtedly well-tried powers of persuasion. He had been quite matter-of-fact about what he wanted to do and why he wanted to do it. He had been tactful and considerate. Never, for one moment, had she feared that he would so much as lay a finger on her. She had been swept along on a kind of inexplicable impluse, almost as if drawn by some invisible and powerful magnet. And now, belatedly, in the solitary tranquillity of her room, she felt shocked and appalled at what she had done.

Her father would certainly not have understood, let alone condoned, her behaviour. He would think that his cherished daughter had abandoned all her principles and fallen prey to the corruption of the big city. And yet, the whole episode had seemed, at the time, to be entirely innocent, based on a mutual trust and respect. Once she had agreed to pose for Michael, she had felt no qualms or reservations about her decision until it was all over. And it had been very nice of him, she reasoned, to explain about the release form. She would, undoubtedly, have signed it out of ignorance, having no knowledge of such legalities. It would not have occurred to her, in her naîveté, to demand any right of veto over the publication of the photographs.

Publication! Why had she not fully considered the implications of this? She had a sudden vivid picture of Michael's book on the shelves of the Auchterbrae mobile library. There she would be, without a stitch on, immortalised for all to see – Douglas, Fiona Sinclair, her father, her old school chums ... surely they would recognise her? What on earth would they think? And what about Sarah? Sarah had called her 'straitlaced' only that morning. What would she make of such an unlikely shedding of inhibitions? 'What you mean is, *you* fancy him!' Sarah had said, cynically. She would be quick to read all kinds of sexual connotations into it. Why had all this not occurred to her at the time? When would she ever learn to look before she leapt?

He *had* manipulated her! Ingeniously, very cleverly, neatly precluding any future recriminations on her part. Oh, he was an expert, all right. It must have been like taking sweets from a baby!

But then again, on the other hand, she could still refuse to sign the form, and demand that the pictures be destroyed. He had given her an out. Had he but known it, an unnecessary one, because it had not been this concession which had swayed Lisa's decision. She had acted, she knew, out of a mixture of pride, faith, and sheer Campbell audacity.

Lisa sighed. She was used to getting herself into scrapes. It was, admittedly, the story of her life. She would review the situation when she saw the pictures. Insomnia was not one of her vices. Curling up, she went to sleep.

Being blessed with a youthful resilience, Lisa put the incident behind her and, flush with her £50, spend a busy week stocking up Sarah's freezer. It had occurred to her that when business started to roll in thick and fast, a supply of ready-made desserts, pâtés and soups would save time and panic. She realised how fortunate she was to be living in a flat with such a well-equipped kitchen. Although it in no way emulated the showroom perfection of the one at Montpelier Gardens, it was bright, practically designed and spacious, with plenty of working surfaces.

Sarah's flat was heavily subsidised. Her father had purchased it outright, and charged his daughter and her flat-mate rent which, by London standards, could only be regarded as nominal. Lisa had met him only once, soon after she moved in. Dapper and suave, he looked to have a devastating bedside manner, in marked contrast to

49

Dr Campbell's gruff, no-nonsense approach. His one great weakness was his daughter, whom he had always spoiled quite shamelessly, and he was clearly pleased, not to say relieved, at Lisa's arrival, seeing her as a good influence on the flighty Sarah, and someone who would encourage her to eat properly. Yes, thought Lisa, rolling pastry, but for Dr Forsyth, she would undoubtedly be ensconced in a dreary hostel somewhere − lights out at eleven, queues for the bathroom and a battleaxe warden. Nothing less would have appeased her father.

She felt a certain devilment, knowing that he had so little insight into her new environment and the characters who peopled it. How he would have snorted at Sarah's diets! How outrageous he would have found Richard's posturing! And what a stern talking-to he would have given Barbara Bentley on the evils of drink. She felt a stab of homesickness for the gentleness, the honesty, the integrity of the people of Auchterbrae, but this was quickly superseded by her excitement at her forthcoming expedition to Lynford Bassett, with six new guests to be impressed, all of them wealthy no doubt, and disinclined to cook for themselves.

She was, despite herself, disappointed not to hear from Michael in the course of the following week. Like many top professionals, he did not do his own darkroom work, but even so, she would have expected a call by now to invite her to inspect the prints. She was more than a little anxious to view the finished product, out of a mixture of curiosity and apprehension. She had little concept of what the pictures would look like, being ignorant of camera angles, the type of lenses used, or the effects of the lighting. She surmised that perhaps Michael was away on an assignment somewhere, photographing more intriguing subject matter than Lisa Campbell.

With a disconcerting shaft of clarity, Lisa realised that,

on and off, she had been thinking about Michael Delaney rather a lot: reviewing what she knew of his history, reflecting on just what made him tick, reliving the brief touch of his hands, the penetrating sensation of his eyes on hers. Ridiculous, she chided herself. She was in danger of becoming star-struck. Even by London standards, Michael Delaney was successful, sought-after, and nobody's fool. Whereas, even by Auchterbrae standards, Lisa was, she knew only too well, one of nature's innocents.

The big day came, and Lisa duly caught the 10.15 to Southampton, arriving at 11.30. Howard Bentley was waiting to meet her train, and ushered her into a large Mercedes. He was extremely friendly and courteous, thanking her for coming so far, and explaining that the lunch party was quite informal – just some neighbours who also had second homes in the district.

'We often come down here for long weekends in the spring and summer,' he told her. 'Barbara gets claustrophobic in town, and of course the fresh air's good for the boy. Mike's very flexible about it – he usually has James on Saturdays, and so while we're here he'll often come down on a Friday night and stay at the Lynford Billet.'

Lisa was somewhat surprised to be given all this detail, but Howard seemed to feel that he owed her some background information after the fracas of the previous Saturday.

'In London,' he continued, 'we live in Holland Park. We have an au pair and a cook-cum-housekeeper, but of course good domestic staff are terribly difficult to come by these days. We had a bit of bother with Mrs Duckett last weekend and Barbara gave her her cards. That's why we're so grateful you were able to help us out.' From the tone of his voice, Lisa got the impression that Mrs

51

Duckett was not the first housekeeper to depart the Bentley household at short notice.

'I hope you won't think me indiscreet,' went on Howard, uncertainly, 'but I think I ought to explain that my wife is going through rather a ... bad patch at the moment. A bit run down, you know. As soon as I can get away from the office I'm planning to take her abroad for a holiday. Give her a break, and so on. I don't want to burden you with our family affairs but, well, I'd just ask you to be ... er, *patient* with her. She does tend to have a rather unfortunate manner sometimes. You mustn't take it personally. I thought it fairer to explain.'

Reading accurately between the lines, Lisa felt touched by Howard's loyal and awkward circumlocution of his wife's drink problem. His harassed, chubby face was faintly pink with embarrassment.

'Don't worry about a thing,' Lisa reassured him. 'It's all in the day's work for me. What a lovely bit of country,' she observed cheerfully. Howard smiled gratefully and changed the subject.

The Bentleys' weekend cottage at Lynford Bassett was a converted farmhouse, luxuriously renovated and refurbished. Barbara, Howard explained, was having a lie-in, but would be getting up any minute. He took Lisa's coat, showed her into an oak-beamed parlour, poured her a glass of sherry and disappeared.

Lisa was anxious to install herself in the kitchen and set about her business. If lunch was to be at one, there was no time to be wasted. After five minutes of twiddling her thumbs, her impatience got the better of her. Abandoning her sherry, she went in search of her temporary domain, if only to preheat the oven. She was standing in the hallway, getting her bearings, when a knowing little voice said, 'You're Lisa. My dad told me about you.'

She started, to see James, looking uncannily like his

52

father, watching her from the top of the narrow staircase.

'Barbara says I'm to show you the kitchen,' he announced gravely, descending purposefully. He took her hand and pulled her along behind him, as if she were a dog on a lead. Bemused, she followed him into a beautiful country kitchen – quarry-tiled floor, oak cabinets, an Aga cooker, and a huge scrubbed wooden table in the centre. Lisa gasped. The kitchen of her dreams!

James opened the fridge and pointed.

'Smoked salmon for starters. Strawberries and cream for pudding. Roast beef. Vegetables in the rack. I'm to set the table for you. Brigitta's at church. Barbara's got period pains,' he continued, 'and Howard's gone to the off-licence.'

Having said his piece, he sat down at the table, chin on hands, and studied her closely. Lisa was quite nonplussed. He wasn't like a child at all, more like a scaled-down adult, with the same piercing, unnervingly black eyes as Michael. Having no siblings, Lisa wasn't used to children. The ones in her home village were the usual noisy, cheeky, unsophisticated variety. This child looked likely to hold his own at a cocktail party.

Smoked salmon and strawberries. There was hardly anything for her to do, apart from putting the beef in the oven, cooking the vegetables, and making the gravy. Lisa was disappointed. This was poor opportunity to demonstrate her culinary skills to a captive audience. The strawberries would, in any case, be imported, tasteless and woollen. Lisa had half a mind to raid the larder and change the menu, but thought better of it. It wouldn't pay to risk implying criticism of Barbara's choice of meal.

She set to, peeling potatoes. She wasn't at all sure what to say to James. The normal 'And what do you want to be when you grow up?' line of questioning seemed entirely inappropriate.

'Your father told me you liked cold roast potatoes,' she remarked, with a flash of inspiration.

James perked up. 'Yes,' he confirmed. 'With tomato sauce.'

An analytical silence ensued, the small black eyes boring into the back of Lisa's head.

'Did you see your dad yesterday, then?' she ventured at length, clutching at straws.

'Of course,' said James, obviously regarding this as rather a silly question. 'We went to see Lynford Rovers,' he added, taking pity on her. 'They lost, 4 - 1. Their goalie's useless.'

Knowing nothing whatsoever about football, Lisa was flummoxed again. 'Do you play yourself?' she asked uncertainly.

'Not properly,' replied James mournfully. 'But they're sending me to Cheltenham next year. Dad says I'll get to play there. And rugby. And cricket.' He brightened visibly at the prospect.

'Do you like your school?' asked Lisa.

'No,' responded James emphatically. 'It's soppy. Miss Gibbons is a silly old cow.'

'That's not a very nice thing to say,' reprimanded Lisa.

James chortled unexpectedly. 'Sorry,' he apologised cheerfully. 'Dad said I wasn't to show him up. I promised him I wouldn't say any rude words. He told me you'd get upset.'

Lisa felt herself colouring furiously. The thought of Michael discussing her with this precocious little beast was really too much.

'He's quite right,' she stated crisply, without turning from the sink. 'Where I come from, children mind their manners. Will you kindly set the table for me now, please? And wash your hands first.'

James strolled over to the sink condescendingly.

54

Evidently he had cultivated his own unique blend of insolence and obedience.

He disappeared unhurriedly into the wood-panelled dining-room, and neatly transferred the contents of the sideboard on to the mahogany table. Inspecting his handiwork some ten minutes later, Lisa had to admit that he'd done an excellent job, and told him so. He accepted her praise impassively, and silently set about setting three further places at the kitchen table, presumably for Lisa, Brigitta and himself.

Lisa soon had the meal under control, working deftly under James's watchful scrutiny. A sort of companionable silence had evolved between them. She didn't wish to incur his contempt with obviously patronising small talk. Retrieving her sherry from the living-room, she sat down at the kitchen table to enjoy it. James was engrossed by this time in a rather lurid comic.

She looked up as Howard returned, bearing a plastic carrier bag. 'Sorry I was so long,' he remarked apologetically, stacking several bottles of tonic water into the fridge. 'Isn't Barbara down yet?'

'I've been up for ages,' snapped Barbara, appearing at the doorway in a peach silk negligée. 'I've been doing my face.' She turned to Lisa and flashed her a brilliant, if rather brittle, smile. 'So glad you could come. Would you be a perfect angel and rustle up some coffee? Instant will do. I need to take some codeine. The old tummy cramps. Where's Brigitta?' she demanded. 'That girl spends so much time in Church she must be angling for a sainthood.'

She accepted the coffee graciously and sat down wearily at the table.

'Jamie, darling, be a good boy and fetch my handbag. My pills are in it.' James complied dutifully with an air of silent martyrdom. 'Thank you, sweetheart,' she cooed, as he returned with a Gucci clutch purse, regaling him with rather excessive kisses on both cheeks. James squirmed. Lisa had the feeling that this display of affection was somewhat stage-managed for her benefit. Barbara ran her fingers through James's hair with exaggerated maternal care. He endured this patiently, scampering back to his comic at the first opportunity.

'Are you sure you're up to it, Babs?' queried Howard gently. 'I can tell them you're not well. Lisa could bring you a tray in your room.'

'I'm perfectly all right,' rapped Barbara, lighting a cigarette. 'I won't have that bitch Pamela Lawrence asking if I've got a hangover.'

Lisa was shocked to hear such language used in front of a child, but James didn't bat an eyelid. Doubtless he had heard much worse. The air of mounting tension was broken by the breathless arrival of the au pair, Brigitta, a teutonic-looking, well built girl, rosy-cheeked and rather heavy on her feet.

'So sorry I arrive late,' she excused herself. 'I have stayed to make my confession.'

'An excellent idea,' remarked Barbara dryly and glided off to get dressed, Howard following in her wake. James, seeming to take exception to the intrusion of Brigitta, removed himself and his comic to the garden. Brigitta held out her hand to Lisa gravely.

'I am so pleased to meet you,' she announced, with Germanic formality. 'I am glad you have come today. Frau Bentley does not like my cooking.' She grimaced comically. 'Soon I return to Munich,' she continued, with an air of some relief. 'Your family are in England?'

'Scotland,' corrected Lisa, aware that Brigitta was unlikely to appreciate the distinction.

'You have a fiancé?' asked Brigitta, going straight to the point. Lisa shook her head, astonished to be thus

56

interrogated after such a brief acquaintance. 'Me, I have a fiancé,' Brigitta informed her with great complacency. 'He makes his military service. Next year, we marry each other.'

'That's nice,' muttered Lisa, suppressing a smile.

'In Bavaria,' continued Brigitta, warming to her theme, 'divorce is not yet the custom. Not like here in England.'

'Oh, I don't know,' protested Lisa mildly, somewhat appalled at Brigitta's bland generalisation. 'It's surely not all that common.'

'Truly,' Brigitta assured her, nodding sagely. 'Both Mr and Mrs Bentley. And Mr Wainwright. And Mrs Lawrence. Four out of eight here to lunch today.'

'Oh really,' acknowledged Lisa, unable to comment further in the face of such statistics.

'Mr Wainwright, he is not yet married again. Mrs Bentley likes him very much. He comes often visiting.' Brigitta winked conspiratorially. Lisa was thankful James had left the room.

'Well, London people are a bit different,' observed Lisa firmly. 'In my home town in Inverness-shire, people tend to stay married.'

'This is good,' approved Brigitta. 'Why do you not have a fiancé? How old are you?'

'Twenty-one,' replied Lisa, slightly defensively, choosing to neglect the first question.

Brigitta clucked sympathetically. 'So you come to England to find a husband, yes?'

'Certainly not,' declared Lisa, torn between amusement and irritation. Brigitta shrugged philosophically, and realising that Lisa was not disposed to discuss the matter further, launched into a long monologue encompassing her own wedding plans, her family in Munich, and, more interestingly, the vagaries of the Bentley ménage.

'Mrs Duckett, she got the sack,' she recounted, with some relish. 'Me, I am glad. She was, how you say, an old cow.' Lisa had an uneasy feeling that Brigitta had picked this idiom up from James rather than the other way round. 'She was sometimes drinking Mrs Bentley's gin,' clarified Brigitta, as if this explained everything. 'Once, James, he put a caterpillar in her bed.' Lisa could believe that.

'Is James very naughty, then?' she could not resist asking.

Brigitta pursed her mouth reflectively. 'He is . . . a difficult child,' she decided, lost for a more descriptive word. Her vocabulary obviously did not stretch to verbal analysis of the enigmatic James. 'He is not content. He prefers his own father, Mr Delaney, I think. Mrs Bentley . . . '

The doorbell rang. Brigitta peeped out of the window and patted her hair. 'Mr Wainwright,' she informed Lisa brightly, and rushed off to answer the door.

'Hello Brigitta, *mein Liebchen*,' came a smooth, oily voice from the hall. Mr Wainwright peered curiously into the kitchen.

'Ah,' he exclaimed lasciviously, 'a new face.'

'How do you do?' muttered Lisa awkwardly, extending her hand with dignity. Mr Wainwright was tall, thin, sandy-haired, expensively clad, and redolent of male cologne. He flashed Lisa a crooked, rakish smile.

'Well, well,' he commented huskily, while Brigitta looked on sullenly, 'you're certainly an improvement on Mrs Duckett.'

Lisa was spared the necessity of repartee by the timely appearance of Barbara, looking absolutely stunning in peacock blue. Much to Lisa's consternation, she kissed Mr Wainwright full on the mouth.

'Hello, Steve darling,' she greeted him throatily. 'Come and have a drink,' and she bore him off. Brigitta

58

gave Lisa a knowing look as Howard came trundling down the stairs. Lisa felt increasingly sorry for him. He looked in amiably.

'Everything going according to plan?' he asked Lisa genially. 'The others will be arriving any minute. I should think we'll be ready to start eating in about half an hour.'

Lisa nodded. She supposed she ought to be glad of the cabaret. Gastronomically, this engagement was a bore.

Three more rings at the doorbell and the complement of guests was complete. Lisa noted that the odd, unpartnered female guest, to counterbalance Steve Wainwright, was a middle-aged dowager-duchess type, evidently hand-picked to present no competition.

The meal, of course, went like clockwork. Once Lisa had cleared away the main course, she, Brigitta and James sat down to eat their own lunch. James, as Michael had warned her, had an amazing appetite for his size. That there were any potatoes left to eat cold was a source of some relief. He didn't have a great deal to say for himself during the meal, concentrating on the serious business of eating. Predictably, Brigitta did most of the talking, her lop-sided English phraseology causing James to raise his eyes silently to heaven once or twice in a disconcertingly adult way. Clearly, he clocked in to everything, even when he affected not to be listening. Lisa, letting Brigitta's prattle wash over her, watched James covertly with growing fascination. When he grew up, she thought, he would be every bit as lethal as his father.

While the guests got stuck in to their liqueurs and coffee, Brigitta loaded the dishwasher, while Lisa restored the kitchen to perfect order. She wasn't quite sure when she was supposed to leave, dependent as she was on Howard taking her to the station. Her duty done, Brigitta excused herself, having arranged to meet a fellow

59

au pair in the village. After she had gone, James asked unexpectedly, 'Are you going to come again?'

'Perhaps,' said Lisa guardedly, 'if your mummy needs help.'

'I don't call Barbara Mummy,' he corrected her. 'She says it makes her feel a hundred years old. Do you have any brothers or sisters?'

'No,' smiled Lisa, shaking her head.

'I don't either,' he informed her unnecessarily. 'Barbara says I'm enough of a handful as it is.'

'But I expect you've got lots of friends at school, haven't you?' prompted Lisa encouragingly.

'Sort of. But they're all a bit wet,' complained James. 'It won't be so bad at Cheltenham, Howard says. Howard went there.' He grimaced slightly. 'Dad says I'll like it. He says it's better than the school he went to. Dad says I can come to live with him when I'm grown up, if I still want to.'

Lisa found these deadpan statements strangely heart-rending.

'Don't you like living with Howard and Barbara?' she asked, amazed at her own candour. It wasn't really the sort of question one asked the child of a broken home.

'They're okay,' conceded James generously. 'But Barbara's always tired. And she cries a lot. And Howard's always busy reading.'

'Well, that's only natural,' pointed out Lisa. 'He's a publisher.'

'My dad's a photographer,' James told her proudly, obviously bored at the subject of Howard and Barbara. 'He's been in ever so many wars, taking pictures.' To Lisa's horror, James started making realistic machine-gun noises, aiming at random all over the kitchen with a ferocious imaginary weapon.

'Stop that at once, James,' reprimanded Lisa. She had

always disapproved of toy guns and war-based games. 'Your daddy's pictures are meant to show how horrible war is. People get hurt, get killed.'

'I know all *that*,' replied James witheringly. 'My dad nearly died, didn't he.' It was a statement, not a question. Lisa wondered if this could be some sort of morbid schoolboy exaggeration, although she couldn't see Michael actively encouraging such a delusion.

'It's true,' elaborated James, patiently, sensing her scepticism. 'He was in hospital for weeks and weeks when I was little. You should see his scars,' he added proudly. 'When he takes me swimming, people stare. Are you staying for tea? Can I have egg and chips?'

Lisa suppressed a sudden fierce urge to pick him up and hug him very tight.

'I don't think so, this time,' she said. 'But if I come again, I'll see what I can do.'

For the first time, she experienced the gratification of James's rare and very special smile. Like Michael's it was totally devastating.

Soon after four o'clock, Lisa thought she had better visit the living-room to offer more coffee. Barbara was chatting vivaciously to Steve Wainwright, only her heightened colour and the brightness of her eyes indicating any possible excess of alcohol.

'Lisa, dear,' she broke off 'we'd all like to thank you for a perfectly super lunch.' A chorus of confirmatory mutterings ensued from the other guests. 'Howard – ' she turned to her husband, her tone a practised combination of the peremptory and the coaxing – 'hadn't you better make sure that Lisa catches the 4.45? We don't want to keep her too terribly late, do we?'

Howard leapt up obediently from his inevitable position entertaining the dowager duchess, and joined Lisa in the hall as she was putting on her coat.

'Mike said you charged £7.50 an hour,' he mentioned casually, 'but of course this is Sunday so we'd expect to pay extra. Then there's your travelling time, and train fare.' He began writing a cheque on the telephone table. 'Don't worry, it shouldn't bounce,' he smiled, feebly attempting a joke. Remembering Michael's parting strictures to her, Lisa thought resolutely of the silver cutlery, heavy crystal, and Barbara's couture dress, shutting her eyes to hide her guilt as she allowed Howard to name a truly exorbitant sum, and trying to look as if she made this kind of money every day of the week.

'We're really most appreciative,' mumbled Howard.

'My pleasure,' beamed Lisa, feeling a regular con-merchant.

Howard opened the front door. Lisa looked round to say goodbye to James, but he seemed to have disappeared.

Howard didn't talk much on the way to the station, driving extra slowly and carefully, no doubt fearing the breathalyser. As he let her out of the car, he said, 'I do hope we can make this a regular thing, Lisa. Perhaps you can come down for the whole weekend sometime? Barbara loves having house parties, but it does mean a lot of extra work, and even if we manage to replace Mrs Duckett, well, you know how it is. There's something about cooking that seems to bring out the temperamental streak in staff, whereas you — you're so calm. No broken crockery, no burnt offerings . . .'

Lisa shook his hand.

'I'd love to come again, Mr Bentley. But, if you could explain it tactfully to your wife for me, smoked salmon and strawberries don't exactly tax my skills. If she'd like to consult me on menus beforehand, I could give her a list of foods to be delivered.'

'No problem, no problem,' enthused Howard. 'I'm

sure Barbara would be more than delighted to give you a free hand. Anything domestic bores her stiff.'

Lisa daydreamed her way back to London, alternately smiling and frowning to herself as she reviewed her first encounter with the diminutive adult who had stolen her heart.

Chapter Four

One sunny afternoon in May Lisa heard, at last, from Michael. His voice over the telephone was dry, casual.

'Are you ready to come over and censor the prints?' he asked sardonically. 'Then we can go off and do the outdoor stuff. The light should be about right by the time we get to Box Hill.'

After secretly chafing at how long it had taken for him to contact her, Lisa felt distinctly bloody-minded.

'As it happens, I'm in the middle of something right now,' she prevaricated.

'No you're not. You're just playing silly bu − hard to get, as usual.' Lisa could not help smiling. No wonder he'd told James not to use any rude words. He'd probably taught him most of them!

'Grab yourself a cab like a good girl. And don't forget your red pencil. I don't happen to possess one,' and he rang off.

Lisa had been just about to ask what she ought to wear, but bit her tongue just in time. His private studio was one thing, but if he seriously thought that she was going to cavort starkers all over Box Hill, he had another think coming! Nevertheless, curiosity soon had her heading in a taxi for Montpelier Gardens. She wanted to see the pictures. Almost as much as she wanted to see Michael.

The plate glass portals clicked open immediately she pressed his buzzer, and the door of number 28 was already ajar. She wrinkled her nose as she entered. There was an unmistakable scent of heady French perfume lingering in the air. No doubt expensive-smelling women were in and out of this place likes bees visiting a hive.

'In here,' he called from the living-room. He was lying full length on one of the settees, hands behind his head, grinning all over his face. She sat down stiffly opposite him.

'A drink?' he queried hospitably, without moving. 'A nice cup of tea, perhaps?'

'No thank you. I'm a bit pressed for time.'

'Aha, uptight as ever, are we? So terribly prim and proper, everything a big favour, no sense of humour, the dour wee Scot with a vengeance ...' His lips were twitching with mischief.

'I *do* have a sense of humour,' bit back Lisa. 'Not one like yours, though. Your idea of fun is just taking a rise out of people, especially me, it seems. And anyway,' she pouted, 'I was never any good at smart backchat.'

His face softened. 'How did it go at Lynford Bassett? Did Babs get up in time for lunch?'

'It went very well,' replied Lisa curtly. 'They want me to go back and cater for weekend house parties.'

'Oh, jolly dee. Very Noel Coward. How civilised, doing the old wife-swapping all under one roof.'

Lisa stood up, glared, then, catching the mockery in his eyes, sat down again.

'And what did you think of Jamie? Did he give you a hard time?'

'I thought he was very like you. Except that he was a lot nicer to me than you are.'

'I'm glad to hear it. But then, unlike me, he's been brought up to have all the social graces. In fact, social

65

graces are all they seem to teach at that namby-pamby school Barbara sends him to.'

'He did say it was a bit soppy,' Lisa couldn't help but smile at the memory of it. 'He's looking forward to going to Cheltenham.'

'So he says,' said Michael, non-committally. 'Well, what do you think of yourself?'

'I beg your pardon?'

'Your pictures.'

'I don't know until I see them, do I?'

For reply, Michael made a broad gesture with his arm around the room, like a circus ringmaster bringing on the next act. Only then did she realise that the photographs which had lined the walls had been removed to be replaced by enlarged lustre prints of a woman whom she might not immediately have recognised: herself.

While Michael lay there watching her, she walked round the room slowly, inspecting them one by one. Soft-focussed, romantic, delicate, lyrical ... could that radiant creature with the mysterious smile, the luminous eyes, the fluid, sensual curves, really be Lisa Campbell? This woman was a nymph, a sprite, a pagan goddess even. The sound of the shutter must have mesmerised her; she had no memory of turning, bending, lifting her head, raising her arms, as she must have done. Had he hypnotised her, or what? And she had expected to look stiff, awkward! She stared at herself so long and so hard that she realised with a jolt that he must think her narcissistic. She turned towards him, slightly dazed.

'You're brilliant, aren't you?' she said artlessly. He seemed unmoved by the compliment.

'And you're beautiful,' he replied simply. The silence vibrated. Lisa sat down.

'Right then,' she said brightly, anxious to break it. 'I'll be signing that form now, and then I must be off.'

66

'Not until I've done the colour shots.'

'Oh, I wanted to have a word with you about those, actually,' she began, haltingly. 'I mean, I'm really not at all happy about doing this sort of thing out of doors. You see – '

'I know, you catch cold easily.'

'I think you've got quite enough pictures there to be going on with,' continued Lisa doggedly.

'And it looks like rain,' he mocked.

They were back to their old battle positions. Lisa looked at him mutinously, but found that the bored, patient expression he wore so reminded her of James's that, despite herself, she suddenly burst out laughing. He didn't ask her to explain her reaction, but the atmosphere immediately lightened and once Lisa had composed herself, Michael explained: 'The outdoor shots are going to be in colour, as I said – it's the effect of your hair and eyes I'm after this time. I visualised you in a very simple, rather old-fashioned white dress. I used Richard's fashion contacts to track down the sort of thing I wanted. Don't worry, your name wasn't mentioned. It's lying on the bed if you'd like to go and put it on.'

Lisa breathed a sigh of relief. 'How did you know my size?' she asked, before colouring at the naîveté of the question.

He smiled tactfully. 'I think you'll find it fits,' he assured her.

It did. It was made of the finest white cotton lawn, trimmed with broderie anglaise, high-necked, long-sleeved, with a close-fitting bodice and a flowing skirt. He gave her five minutes to change, and knocked before coming in.

Lisa's hair, as on a normal working day, was coiled up on top of her head to keep it out of the way while she was cooking. Standing behind her as she faced the full-length mirror, Michael coolly set about removing all the pins, dropping them wordlessly, one by one, on to the bedside table.

'Do you have a hairbrush?' he asked. She fumbled obediently in her handbag and produced the small bristle brush she carried eveywhere for fast taming of her thick, unruly tresses. Gently, he began to brush her hair back from her face with long, sweeping strokes, his left hand on her shoulder. The brush moved rhythmically to and fro, the bristles making her scalp tingle. Unaccountably, the tingling sensation started to invade other parts of her body. She stood very still, not daring to catch his eye in the mirror, fearful of revealing the disturbing, subtle sense of arousal he was provoking. Then, with the dexterity of a hairdresser, he parted her hair in the middle and spread it in front of her shoulders, the red glowing against the snowy whiteness of the dress.

'Bring it with you,' he said impassively, handing the brush back to her. 'It gets a bit blowy up on Box Hill.'

A dark green Volvo estate was standing in a resident's parking bay not far from the flat. He had already loaded it with the equipment he needed. The car was luxurious, an automatic model with leather upholstery, the engine virtually silent, the electric windows of smoked glass.

'This is a nice car,' remarked Lisa artlessly. She herself had been until recently the proud possessor of a beaten-up Morris 1100, and the flashiest car in the village was Douglas's Ford Capri.

'It's extremely practical,' he smiled, 'although Jamie doesn't rate it. He sees me in something more macho, like a Porsche. Better for pulling birds, no doubt, but this is much more comfortable, don't you think?' His eyes sparkled with mischief. Lisa decided that she'd better get used to being ribbed by him all the time, besides which, she was finding it increasingly difficult to stay cross with

68

him for more than a few minutes at a time. She resolved to give as good as she got, and started to sniff the air exaggeratedly.

'What's the matter? I have a bath every week, you know.'

'The perfume,' said Lisa sweetly. 'This smells like Chanel Number 5. But I could have sworn the one back in your flat was Miss Dior. I think the Miss Dior suits you better, actually. Tell me, do you dab it behind your ears, or splash it on your wrists?'

'Aren't we a witty body today? And what do you use? Midnight in Aberdeen?'

'How did you guess? Pity you've missed my birthday by a month, or you could have bought me a big bottle.'

'Aha! Then you must be an Aries. What a coincidence, so am I. And do you go rushing in where angels fear to tread?'

'Of course. Let's see: I'm impatient, impulsive, quick-tempered, intolerant, reckless . . .' parrotted Lisa, quoting the popular horoscope epithets ' . . . but that's nothing to do with being an Aries. It's to do with being a Campbell.'

'An Aries Campbell with red hair. God help us! You're enough to make a strong man shake, aren't you? And how old would you be, little Miss Aries?'

'Twenty-one.' Lisa giggled. 'Brigitta thinks I'm on the shelf. She asked me if I'd come down south to find myself a man.'

'Ah yes, the winsome Brunhilde. You want to hear Jamie taking off her accent. Yours'll be next, you wait. He's a born mimic.'

'Do you see him every week?'

'Except when I'm away somewhere. Saturdays, mostly. He's a football fanatic. Usually we watch West Ham, when they're at home.'

'He talks about you all the time.'

'Absence makes the heart grow fonder. He associates me with outings, treats, having a good time. I don't have to nag him about washing behind his ears or it being past his bedtime. Babs cops all that side of it. So, understandably, he's going through a phase of thinking I'm Superman. I've explained all that to Barbara umpteen times, but she's developed a fixation that he prefers me to her. Says he doesn't love her any more and so on. Some innocent remark someone made about children is what got her going at the party.

'The pity of it is, the more obsessed she gets about it, the more Jamie withdraws from her. She tends to come over a bit maudlin when she's sozzled, starts slobbering over him. He doesn't like it. As for poor old Howard, well, he does his best, but it's a thankless task, getting lumbered with another bloke's kid. Still, Jamie can take it. He's a tough little nut.'

Privately, Lisa wondered just how much well-hidden vulnerability there was in the redoubtable James, thinking back wistfully to the tranquil security of her own childhood.

'Why is Barbara so unhappy?' she asked, her inherent candour emerging as she relaxed. 'Is she still in love with you?'

'That's a very personal question, isn't it?'

'I know it is. You told me to start acting naturally. I happen to be extremely nosy.'

'Touché. No, of course she's not still in love with me – assuming, of course, that she ever was. It wasn't me that drove her to the booze, in case that's what you're thinking. She could drink a navvy under the table long before she ever met me. Howard's been very good for her, he's kept her dry for weeks at a time, but she's going through one of her bad spells at the moment. Why the hell

70

are we discussing Barbara, anyway? I'm sure you don't really want to hear all this.'

'Yes I do. Does she love Howard?'

'You're very hot on love, aren't you? I suppose in your vocabulary it's a nice cut and dried word. Try defining it, Lisa. What does it mean?'

'Oh, love is ... caring, trusting, needing, wanting, sharing ...'

He cut her short, not taking his eyes from the road.

'Very nice. You just keep believing all that, Lisa. For as long as life lets you.' His voice had turned hard again. What an unpredictable man he was!

'Well,' she countered boldly, 'you tell me what you think it means.'

'Not right now,' said Michael. 'Not until I've taken the pictures.'

By the time they got to Box Hill, these touchy subjects had been firmly shelved. Instead, Michael had set himself to entertain her, his irreverent line in patter reducing her effortlessly to frequent, helpless mirth. Evidently he had not shed his East End wit along with his accent.

'You could talk the hind leg off a donkey,' Lisa informed him, having just been seduced into laughing at something she would normally have considered in rather dubious taste.

'Very useful when I want a picture of a three-legged mule,' he grinned, parking the car.

His photographic equipment was a lot less intimidating this time — a hand-held motor-driven Nikon and several heavy-looking lenses. He took the trouble to explain to her, in very simple language, what their different functions were, and then told her to hurry up, the light was just how he wanted it. It being rather chilly, despite the sunshine, there were not many people about, and they had no difficulty in finding a suitable stretch of deserted hillside.

71

'Lie down,' he said. Carefully, he arranged her hair around her face. It glinted red in the mellow sunlight against the lush green grass and the white cotton. Standing over her, his legs either side of her hips, he seemed gigantic. Lisa looked up helplessly at her own image, reflected darkly in the deep blue-blackness of the zoom lens. Before she had time to tense up, Michael said casually from somewhere behind the viewfinder, 'Tell me how you make an omelette, Lisa.'

'An ome-' click '-lette?'

'That's right.'

'Well, you break the eggs into a basin, and – '

'Into a what?'

'A ba-' click '-sin. And then you beat them with a fork.'

'What, not an electric whisk?'

'*No*.' Click. 'That would spoil the texture. You season the mixture, and take a really hot pan . . .'

She supposed vaguely that this conversation must be to relax her, and so she prattled on, repeating certain words to order. The omelette was folded temptingly on a heated plate by the time Michael changed his film and inserted a different lens. He lay down beside her on the grass.

'Turn towards me, on your side, and close your eyes.' It was true, his voice did have a hypnotic quality. If he'd told her to stand on her head, she would probably have done it.

'Now imagine something nice. Keep your eyes shut.'

'What should I imagine?'

'That's up to you. Whatever turns you on. Rustling palm trees, Robert Redford, haggis . . . '

Lisa opened her eyes and laughed. Click.

'Try again. Something really nice this time. Like being kissed.'

Lisa shut her eyes in a hurry. The lens seemed suddenly uncomfortably close to her face. She tried, obediently, to

72

adopt an expression of sublime content. No click. Michael propped himself up on one elbow.

'No good. Don't you like being kissed? Think of whatever it is you prefer, then.'

His mocking tone put her instantly back on the defensive.

'Of course I like being kissed!' she declared crossly. She shut her eyes again, and re-assumed what she considered to be a sexy, kittenish, dreamy look. She was getting quite good at modelling, she thought. Sarah should look at her laurels.

'If that's the best you can do,' remarked Michael, after a further silence, 'I'm going to have to kiss you myself.'

Lisa sat up. 'You told me you never took advantage of your models,' she reminded him. He was teasing again, of course. She was not inclined to take the threat seriously.

'Don't let your imagination run away with you. I said kiss you, not make love to you. God, you look terrified. It doesn't make you pregnant, you know.'

This was too much. 'Kindly don't patronise me,' stormed Lisa. 'I'm quite well aware of the facts of life, and I – '

Too late. His mouth caught her lips while they were still parted in protest. Very gently, very teasingly, he leaned her back against the grass. It was not a passionate kiss, just a very, very titillating one, one that made resistance seem like over-reaction, one that left the innocent victim hungry for more. A tantalising hors-d'oeuvre of a kiss, designed to sharpen the appetite.

'Cold-blooded swine, aren't I?' he pre-empted her, as, dazed, she heard several consecutive clicks and opened her eyes to a couple more.

'All in a good cause,' he grinned unapologetically. Lisa tried hard to feel a sense of outrage, but it just wouldn't come.

73

'That's it, then,' he announced, standing up. She scrambled to her feet, dusting the blades of grass off her dress.

'There are a few green stains on the back,' he remarked, 'but they'll wash out. You should keep the dress, it suits you.'

He strode back in the direction of the car while she followed at a distance. There was the same sense of anti-climax she'd felt after the session in the studio. This time, though, he wouldn't be taking any more pictures of her. He already had enough for a whole book. He wouldn't be kissing her again, either.

She got back into the car, shivering. There had been a cold wind she hadn't noticed till now. Although she'd worn warm clothes to come out that day, she hadn't, in the deceptive sunshine, brought a coat with her. He must have noticed her discomfort, because without a word he peeled off the sweater he was wearing and tossed it to her as he started the car and looked over his shoulder to reverse out of the parking space.

Lisa pulled it over her head, inhaling the clean, warm, sensual smell of it. It was at least six sizes too big for her.

'Won't you be cold?' she asked, viewing the thin, almost transparent blue shirt, dark with the hair beneath it.

'Nope. What do you want to do this evening, then?'

'This evening? But I thought we'd finished!'

'Oh, I wouldn't put it quite like that. Our photographic contract is over, or almost. Technically speaking, I should pay you a fee for posing for me. It's quite normal and perfectly correct. But if I dare to offer you money, you'll be mortally offended and think it means I regard you as a woman of easy virtue. Right?'

'If you'd offered to pay me at the start,' said Lisa rather loftily, her dignity out of place in the outsize jumper, 'I would have refused to do it.'

74

'Quite so. However, I would like to show my appreciation in some way. Is there anything you'd particularly like to do? I'd suggest going out to dinner somewhere, but I suppose you'd consider that a busman's holiday.'

'You mean, take me out to a restaurant?'

'Well, it's a bit nippy for a picnic, don't you think?'

'But haven't you anything better to do? I mean – '

'You really know how to put a bloke down, don't you? Why don't you just accept graciously? Please, Lisa, I humbly beg you, will you come out with me tonight? Will that do? Cor,' he added, deliberately shifting his vowels, 'I don't usually 'ave all this bovver wiv birds.'

'Well,' said Lisa, hesitantly, 'I've always wanted to go to Leith's.' Prue Leith was one of her idols.

'Great idea. They have a terrific way with duck. Tell you what, we'll just drop this lot off at the lab – it'll be ready in a couple of hours – then I'll take you back to your place so you can get yourself tarted up.' Lisa winced. 'I'll pick you up at about seven. We'll project the pictures and have a couple of jars before dinner. Then we'll go out and have a good guts.' He roared with laughter at Lisa's expression. 'Don't worry. I'll try to remember which knives and forks to use, and I promise not to slurp my soup.'

'You're quite impossible,' scolded Lisa, unable to keep her face straight.

'So people keep telling me,' was the incorrigible reply.

Michael used a lab near Olympia. 'Can you drive?' he asked her abruptly as they approached it.

'Yes,' confirmed Lisa uncertainly, eyeing the traffic. Driving her old banger in the lanes round Auchterbrae required very little expertise.

'Good,' he said. 'This area's running alive with wardens. If I leap out when we get to the lab, you can save me getting a ticket by taking the car round the block. Just keep turning right. There's no left turn, anyway.'

'I can't!' protested Lisa. 'I can only drive a Morris 1100.'

'If you can drive one of those, you can drive anything,' was the casual response. 'This is an automatic. Power steering. A child could drive it.'

'I – I might hit something!'

'That's okay. I'm insured.'

'Stop teasing. I'd be a nervous wreck. This car must be worth a fortune. I wouldn't like to damage it.'

'How delightful it would be,' said Michael, 'to have you in my debt. Here we are. Move over.' And stopping with a sublime disregard for the angry taxi on his tail, he vanished across the street.

Lisa was sweating with fear. Her feet didn't even reach the pedals, and there was a considerable delay while she worked out how to move the seat forward. Gripping the steering wheel for dear life, she managed to move the powerful car to the next junction, tried to indicate right, and promptly switched on the windscreen wipers instead. She hesitated again, causing the irate taxi to hoot furiously. Heartily glad that James wasn't in the car, Lisa quietly and viciously exhausted her limited stock of swear words, but the bit was between her teeth and her pride would not allow her to flunk this new and unexpected ordeal. Her second right rurn was marginally easier, and the third better still. She had just boldly negotiated the fourth, teeth gritted, when she spotted Michael on the nearside pavement, cheerfully making as if to thumb a lift. Ignoring the bus sitting on her bumper, she braked, put the car in neutral, and moved over to the passenger seat, her arms folded menacingly.

'I don't think that was very funny,' she fumed, as Michael pushed the seat back and saluted his thanks to the waiting bus.

'What's the big deal?' he queried mildly. 'Next time

you won't think anything of it.' He flashed her a provocative look. 'There has to be a first time for everything, you know.'

It was just after four when he dropped her outside Rochester Terrace. She was inside the flat before she realised that she was still wearing his sweater. Deciding that she had better put the stained dress to soak right away, she pulled the sweater over her head, and experienced, more intensely this time, the physical essence of him lingering in the borrowed garment. Instinctively, she held it aginst her face. It was some kind of mohair, which tickled her skin. She breathed in deeply. Don't be silly, she chided herself, remembering Sarah's worldly-wise assumption that she fancied Michael. She did, there was no getting round it. But then so did hordes of other women. And he knew it. This outing tonight was to be a one-off date, in lieu of a modelling fee, no more than that. Probably he found her lack of sophistication a novelty, given the glamorous type of female he usually had dealings with.

Of course, one couldn't deny that there was a certain intimacy about having had him take the photographs. But it was, after all, a totally artificial intimacy — ephemeral, impersonal and wholly insignificant. More than likely he was fully expecting her to develop a schoolgirl crush on him, and doubted whether he would even bother to take advantage of it. Why should he mess about making up to a country virgin? More practised women were queuing up for his favours. No, he was just a bit jaded, in need of a quiet evening out with someone who would make no demands on him, someone he felt a bit sorry for. As for that kiss ... she ran her tongue around her lips, remembering it. Like he had said, it had been cold-blooded.

Chapter Five

Getting 'tarted up' involved a trusted green velvet sleeve-
less dress, the best one Lisa possessed, very plain but
starkly effective with her colouring. She was doing rather
a good job on her hair, coiling it up in an elegant evening
style, when Sarah walked in.

'Ooh,' she said, approvingly. 'Going out, are we?'

How inevitable, thought Lisa. The one evening I want
to sneak off without Sarah knowing about it, is the one
evening she shows up early.

'Uh-huh,' she confirmed nonchalantly, her mouth full
of pins.

'Who with?' pursued Sarah ungrammatically.

Lisa shut her eyes, removed the pins, took a deep
breath, and said, 'Michael Delaney.'

Sarah sat down on the bed. 'You mean you're going to
cook for him again?'

'No. He's taking me to Leith's.'

'Why?'

'I didn't ask him why,' replied Lisa succinctly.

'You mean, it's a date?'

'I didn't ask him that either. Why don't you ask him
yourself, if you're so curious. He'll be here in ten
minutes.'

'Well,' exhaled Sarah, obviously impressed. 'You *are* a dark horse.'

Knowing Sarah's propensity for spreading gossip, Lisa relented. 'It isn't a romance, Sarah,' she explained patiently. 'He's just showing his appreciation for – er, what I did for Barbara.'

'Some appreciation. I just wish I'd got to the first-aid kit first. Are you on the pill?'

Lisa stood up and faced her friend squarely. 'Don't be offensive,' she said coldly.

'What do you mean, offensive? Don't be a prig, Lisa. It's just that he'll assume you are. Everyone is, these days.'

'Sarah,' cut in Lisa, eyes flashing. 'Like yourself, I am a doctor's daughter. I am quite familiar with these matters. I am not, however, currently in need of the pill – or any other contraceptive aid, thank you very much. When I am, I've no doubt you'll prove a fount of wisdom on the subject.'

'Hoity-toity,' sulked Sarah. 'Just don't come running to me if you end up in the club. Play it cool by all means, but remember he might not ask you twice. Push him my way when you've finished, won't you?' And, looking very upstaged, Sarah flounced off to her own room.

Lisa was increasingly glad she hadn't confided in Sarah about the photographs. By the time they were published, the two of them would hopefully have gone their separate ways. Was she on the pill indeed? snorted Lisa. The cheek of the woman!

Predictably, it was Sarah who contrived to answer the doorbell, having changed in record time into a black lace negligée.

'Hello, Michael darling,' she purred. 'Didn't get a chance to thank you properly for the super party.'

He had forsaken his usual casual attire in favour of an

79

expensively tailored dark blue suit, set off by a frilled white shirt and an extremely rakish velvet bow tie, an outfit which made him look positively satanic.

'Hello, Sarah,' said Michael in his most seductive voice, eyeing Lisa skulking by her bedroom door. 'Nothing serious, I hope?' He peered closely at her with an air of deep concern.

'Sorry?' tinkled Sarah, completely nonplussed.

'I seem to have got you out of bed to answer the door. So sorry. Not the 'flu, I trust? Treacherous time of year. You should wrap up warmer.'

His eyes undressed her pitilessly. Lisa had never expected to see Sarah blush. It didn't suit her.

'I − er − was just getting changed to go out, actually,' she explained, uncharacteristically flustered.

'Two-timing Richard, eh? Caught you out. I happen to know he's staying down in Penzance overnight on that swimwear job.' Michael wagged his finger accusingly. 'Naughty girl. I've a good mind to tell on you. What's it worth?'

Lisa suppressed a giggle. Sarah certainly wasn't two-timing Richard. If she had been, she would without doubt have regaled Lisa with all the grisly details. No, this was one of Sarah's periodic lazy evenings at home, when she did her toenails in front of the telly with a face-pack on. No wonder she was so put out.

'Come on, gorgeous,' continued Michael, giving Lisa a smouldering look. 'Sarah wants to make herself beautiful for Mr Mystery.' And as Sarah changed from pink to pale green, he put his arm protectively around Lisa and vanished with her down the stairs.

When they were safely out in the street, Lisa gave herself up to rather guilty laughter. Michael kept his arm around her, smiling knowingly as they walked down the Cromwell Road to Montpelier Gardens.

'It's not polite to keep a joke to yourself,' he rebuked her, as she pulled herself together. Lisa knew that he was perfectly well aware of the cause of her hilarity, but she was reluctant to appear catty.

'Let me guess,' he mused with mock gravity. 'She pleaded with you not to risk your virtue, offered to sacrifice herself in your place, and when all else failed, insisted on giving you the name of a *sooper* little abortionist.'

'Michael, really!' exclaimed Lisa, genuinely shocked despite the fact that he had been uncannily near the mark.

'I like it. Say it again.'

'What?'

'Michael. Do you know, you've never once used my name? You've always managed to avoid calling me anything, even Mr Delaney.'

'I hadn't realised,' said Lisa, surprised, 'though now you mention it, it wouldn't have felt right, somehow, calling you Mr Delaney. And I suppose I was . . . shy, of calling you Michael.'

'What, after all we've been through together?' he teased. Despite this veiled reference, however, Lisa didn't, for once, feel embarrassed. In fact, she was already feeling quite perilously relaxed.

On entering his flat she noticed with some relief, that the prints were no longer on the walls, which were now reduced to unadorned whiteness.

'You didn't think I'd leave them up, did you?' he asked quietly, seeing her eyes move. 'One, and one only, will be going in the book. The rest are . . . private. What can I get you to drink? Would you like to try something different? Some wicked cocktail that will remove all your girlish inhibitions?'

'I'll have whatever you're having,' responded Lisa, unabashed.

'Let's have wine, shall we?' he suggested, uncorking a

81

bottle. 'Then we can stick to the same thing all evening. Sit over there, I'm going to project the shots we took this afternoon.' He handed her a glass, switched off the lights, and sat beside her in the darkness, a remote control device in his hand. 'I'm rather pleased with these,' he confessed. 'Beats the back row of the flicks, don't you think?' He pulled her against him so that her head was leaning against his shoulder. It seemed an entirely comfortable place for it to be.

Projected on the white wall, her face was huge in close-up. 'Just look at that skin,' he muttered, as if he were discussing her with someone else. As the shots followed one upon the other, it seemed to Lisa that he had succeeded in capturing the entire repertoire of the positive facial register − surprise, amusement, curiosity, serenity, her mouth and eyes adapting to every nuance of these unconciously expressed moods.

'That's when you made me say "basin!"'' she exclaimed, with a flash of insight, seeing her lips parted wide, her eyes questioning his request.

'You didn't really think I didn't know how to make an omelette, did you?'

The colour composition of white, red and green gave a springlike, pastoral effect, totally without apparent artifice. As he promised, the pictures were not corny. Only the last few images on the roll made her feel uncomfortable. They were the ones he had taken after he had kissed her. She hadn't realised how much her face gave her away. What must he think of her?

'That's the one, I think,' he remarked critically, flashing back to home in on the one particular shot she would rather he discarded. 'Unless, of course, you've finally decided against signing your life away.'

'I'd quite like to get that over with, actually,' said Lisa, putting her glass down and jumping up to switch on the lights. 'Before I change my mind.'

He looked at her carefully for a moment, then got up and fetched a printed form from the desk by the window. He filled in the necessary blanks and then handed it to her, putting a silver pen on the table beside her.

'Read all the small print,' he advised her. 'Basically, you're signing that I can do what I like with them. I don't go in for contracts with exclusion clauses. So, if I hit hard times, you might just end up on a deodorant ad or on one of those calendars in working men's clubs. You'll just have to take that risk.'

'That's okay,' declared Lisa, signing with a flourish. 'I do trust you, you know.'

He sighed. 'Don't sign it just because you trust me. You hardly know me, after all.'

'Are you trying to talk me out of it?' said Lisa, perplexed, holding out the signed form and the pen.

'Perhaps,' he said, cryptically. But he accepted the form and put it away in his desk.

'How did you become a photographer?' she asked boldly, wondering how accurate Sarah's synopsis of his career had been. She half-expected him to duck the question, but he sat back good-naturedly and gave the question some thought.

'Even when I was a kid, that's what I wanted to be. You know how it is at school. All the other little snots were going to be train drivers, or test pilots or professional footballers. I was always going to be a photographer. I got ribbed something chronic. It sounded pretty sissy at the school I went to. Of course, when I left school, the old man was dead set on me getting a trade. They had proper old-fashioned apprenticeships in those days. Seven years it took me to become a fully-fledged brickie. I must have made a few million gallons of tea in that time. Well, it

83

wasn't a bad life. Dad was a lorry driver, earned good money. I only had one sister, Sylvia – she's quite a bit older than me. My mum was a terrific manager and there was always plenty of everything to go round. Popular myth puts it about that I come from a deprived background. Deprived my ar – Aunt Fanny. Typical middle-class inverted snobbery.

'Well, there I was at twenty-three. Sylv was already married with a couple of kids, I was still living in Canning Town with my mum and dad. Plenty of money in my pocket, plenty of . . . social life.' He grinned at his own euphemism. 'I was taking pictures every spare minute. Anything and everything, specially if I thought it would sell. I had this fond ambition to turn pro, you see. I read all the books, mugged up all the technical bumf, touted my stuff like mad round local papers, picture agencies, you name it. Useless. Nobody wanted to know. It's like freelance anything – writing, acting, cooking! You don't get anywhere without that vital first break.

'I don't know how long I would have carried on like that, beating my head against one of my own brick walls, but then, very suddenly, my dad snuffed it – heart, bang, just like that, and the old lady wanted to move out to Essex to be near Sylv. So I threw in the trowel, so to speak, packed up all my gear, and took off. I was heading for Australia to begin with, thought that perhaps the market there might be less saturated. Luckily for me there was a handy war on at the time. All those poor sods didn't die in vain, they made my reputation.' His voice was harsh. 'Cliché or not, war really is sickening, and you genuinely don't realise it when you're sitting at home or relaxing in the pub. That's how I justified my trade to my-self – that I was telling it like it was. Well, that was true, of course.

'By the time my Viet Nam stuff had been plastered all

over the quality press, I was your original working-class hero. Suddenly everyone wanted to know me. That's how I got to meet Barbara. She was knocking around with a big picture editor at the time, and we met at one of those Fleet Street junkets. Are you sure you want to hear all this?' he broke off abruptly. Lisa nodded, fascinated, not wanting so speak and risk interrupting his flow.

'I fell for her like a ton of bricks — quite appropriate don't you think, in my case? She was the most beautiful thing I'd ever clapped eyes on, and, of course, very classy with it. I'd never met anyone like her before. Not only that, she was sensational in bed.

'It was the attraction of opposites, I suppose. Her family certainly thought so. They regarded me as distinctly downmarket, some kind of social gatecrasher. As I said, I'd ditched the accent early on, and I was starting to make a name for myself but, when it comes to class, people are like dogs, they can smell their own kind a mile off, and they definitely didn't rate my pedigree.

'Well, let's just say Babs went for my rough and ready charm, shall we? In no time flat we were married, and James came along soon after. Babs always was very highly strung, but she thought that marrying me and having a baby would cure all her hang-ups. Naturally, it didn't. Before long she got fed up living in a manner to which she'd never become accustomed. We weren't skint, far from it. We had a reasonable little flat in Clapham, and we had the baby she said she wanted so badly. But I realised, too late, that what Babs had really had in mind all along was turning me into some kind of part-time dilettante, photographing debs at parties and the like while we lived beyond our means on a nice fat allowance from Daddy. Just as well Daddy wouldn't come across, because I wasn't having any of it. I wasn't going to let my hard-won reputation slip through my

85

fingers and end up a flaming nine-day wonder.

'It was tough on her, of course it was. There's a war on somewhere in the world all the time. In those three years we were together, I managed to get most of them. I'd warned her right at the start that that was the way it would be, but I guess she didn't want to believe me. James wasn't an easy baby, and Babs couldn't really cope with him. I tried to help whenever I was at home – I got to be a dab hand at changing nappies – but then I was away at least half the time. I was selfish and ambitious, I admit, but in my defence, the marriage would have been doomed anyway.

'We never really had anything in common, apart from sex, and understandably Barbara got ... lonely when I was away, and there were always plenty of shoulders for her to cry on. She was quite honest about it, actually, tended to rub it in. While I was taking my little holiday snaps, up to my neck in the proverbial muck and bullets, she chose to imagine that I was enjoying all kinds of local night-life on the side. In fact, I was never unfaithful to her during those years, but it suited her not to believe me, she still doesn't to this day.' He shrugged.

'One night, I got home after a three-week stint in some godforsaken place to find that Babs had moved home to Mummy and Daddy, taking James with her. They welcomed her with open arms. Can't say I blamed them. Anyway,' he finished briskly, cutting his narrative short with an air of summing up, 'the rest you know. I packed up wars, Babs married Howard, and Bob's your uncle.' He looked at his watch. 'I booked the table for eight-thirty,' he smiled. 'We'd better make a move.'

Lisa suspected that he'd chosen to leave out large and significant chunks of the story, but shrank instinctively from probing further.

'Want to drive?' he teased, opening the passenger door

86

for her and then sliding in beside her. 'Be a sport. After giving you that sob story, I feel like drowning my sorrows. I can get quietly sloshed while I tell you all my troubles, and then you can chauffeur me home and put me to bed.'

'Get away with you,' laughed Lisa, punching him playfully without thinking, before withdrawing her hand hastily. He caught hold of it.

'Remember, I'm not a gentleman,' he cautioned her. 'I hit back.' His hand was dry, warm, with an uncompromising grip. His eyes burned into her face. 'I don't usually dish out my life story,' he mused. 'I feel as if I've just taken all my clothes off. I guess that makes us quits.' He released her hand and started the car.

Lisa had never been to a smart, expensive gourmet restaurant before and was acutely conscious of a lack of savoir-faire. This place was indeed a far cry from the local steak-house back home. But she relaxed quickly. Michael had obviously been there on several occasions and effortlessly secured one of the best tables. Clearly, when it suited him, he could convince anyone that he had been used to elegant living all his life. He displayed an unmistakable air of quiet authority, an indefinable charisma, a practised charm, which he could turn on and off like a tap. Lisa watched him covertly over the top of her menu as he ordered. He wasn't conventionally good-looking, she decided. The face was too lived-in to be described so blandly. Tough, stern, almost menacing-looking, he was physically imposing, powerful, someone you wouldn't choose to tangle with. But when those hard features creased into a smile, she thought, that's when you really had to watch out. Michael had been guilty of untypically false modesty in describing his personal brand of charm as 'rough and ready'. Plainly it was infinitely versatile, kept in tip-top condition, and regularly exercised to ensure it got him everything he wanted. By fair means or, undoubtedly, by foul. Just as well for her that this was essentially an innocent social encounter. Lisa knew her limitations. She would be totally out of her depth with a man like this.

She took a naïve delight in the meal, analysing each dish as to the ingredients and techniques used.

'You're really passionate about your subject, aren't you?' he commented seriously. 'Why didn't you go in for cookery before now?'

'I never really thought of it in terms of a career until just recently,' she explained, 'and now, of course, it's really taken a hold of me. My mother taught me originally. She was a really good, plain cook.'

'Was? She's dead then?'

'Yes. Five years ago. She'd been in bad health for some years, it wasn't unexpected. I was only sixteen, and my father needed help with the practice. Then I just drifted from job to job. I kept getting the sack.'

'The sack? I can't imagine you misbehaving.'

Lisa gave him a rather wicked look. The wine must be going to her head. 'I have an unfortunate tongue. I always say exactly what I'm thinking – not deliberately, it just comes out. It doesn't go down too well when you're the office dogsbody. Apart from that, I'm a bit of a day-dreamer. Anyway, I kept moving on from one dead end job to another, and then one day I realised that I was getting on for twenty-one and I had to do something about it.'

'A great age,' nodded Michael, amused. 'No wonder Brigitta thinks you're past it.'

'Back where I come from,' continued Lisa, picking up his theme, 'people are very marriage-minded. I mean, if you go out with anyone more then a few times, you're practically considered to be engaged! The men are just as bad as the women.'

88

'So you were fed up fending off prospective husbands, eh?'

'Oh, that would be an exaggeration, but I did have quite a few proposals.'

'What an artless way you have of putting things, Lisa. Are they very cold fish, the lusty laddies of Auchterbrae? How did you manage to evade their clutches for so long?'

Lisa thought uncomfortably of the undignified grapples she'd had with some of her bolder admirers. 'Well, you might say I never had any serious temptation. So there's no credit in my virtue really, is there?' she admitted frankly.

'And what if you had been tempted? What then?'

'Then I suppose I'd have had to get married,' said Lisa, with deliberately innocuous glibness. She was getting herself into deep water and she knew it.

'*Had* to get married?' he repeated with mock horror.

'Oh, I didn't mean it that way — as you very well know,' she remonstrated, demolishing the last delicious mouthful of duck.

'Did you enjoy that?' he asked, sitting back and viewing her clean plate with approval. 'Shall we ask for seconds?'

Lisa giggled. He refilled her glass.

'I've had enough wine,' protested Lisa. 'I've already had more than you.'

'You forget, I'm driving,' he reminded her sweetly, pouring himself some Perrier. 'You know, Lisa, you're not going to be safe in this big bad city for very much longer. Your ravishingly genuine innocence brings out the beast in a certain type of man. You are so obviously totally defenceless.'

Lisa sighed. 'You're beginning to sound like Sarah.'

'When it comes to that particular topic, Sarah knows what she's talking about. I wouldn't pooh-pooh all her advice. She's a survivor. She needs to be, in her line of business.'

'Everyone always underestimates me,' complained Lisa petulantly. 'Believe it or not, I can look after myself.'

'Famous last words.'

'Look,' objected Lisa, rising to the bait, 'I'm not Sarah, and I'm not you either, and perhaps I see life differently from both of you. You can call me provincial if you like, but I refuse to be ashamed of being ... innocent, as you put it. Innocence isn't ignorance, just as cynicism isn't wisdom.'

'Good moralistic stuff,' he applauded, clapping his hands mockingly. He was no longer smiling.

'You asked me earlier today,' went on Lisa recklessly, 'to define love. When I did, you delivered some crushing put-down or other, I don't recall it exactly, but you wouldn't tell me what *you* thought it meant. Well, as you know so much about life, why don't you enlighten me with your understanding of the word?' Oh dear, thought Lisa, here I go again, when will I ever learn to keep my big mouth shut?

'Love? What sort? The sort between a man and a woman I suppose? Well, that'll do to start off with. I remember what you said it meant. You said it was caring, trusting, needing, wanting and sharing. I was listening, you see. That's not a bad description of what it ought to be, in an ideal world. Very commendable. In practice, it can mean demanding, withholding, taking, hurting, cheating, lying and punishing.

'When you love a woman, she has absolute power over you. It's like giving her a loaded gun and trusting her not to pull the trigger. Every so often, she might get the gun out and start waving it about a bit. Sometimes she'll fire a few blanks, just to liven things up. Sooner or later, she'll

90

move on to real bullets. Of course, if she loves you too, that means you've got a gun of your own, and you might just start carrying it around with you in self-defence. And then, before you know it, bang, you've got the shoot-out at the O.K. Corral. The moral of the story is, if you're going to marry someone, make sure beforehand that you're both pacifists. Then you might just manage to steer your relationship towards a natural, bloodless death.'

Lisa looked at him scornfully. 'That's the most bitter and twisted thing I've ever heard,' she said. She sounded, even to her own ears, self-righteous.

'I'm not bitter. I just learn by my own mistakes. Quite a healthy habit. One that Barbara should have cultivated. She chases Howard all over both their houses with a sawn-off shotgun. Poor fellow's only got a water pistol to fire back at her.'

'So you'd never get married again?'

'I didn't say that. I said I'm not handing out any more firearms. If I got married again, it would be on a very different basis.'

'You mean, without love?'

'We're back to the dictionary again. I wouldn't marry anyone I didn't find sexually attractive. I wouldn't marry anyone I didn't like as a person. But next time – if there is a next time – I intend it to be painless.'

'Painless? That sounds boring.'

'*That* sounds trite. Your father's a doctor. You can't honestly believe there's a single good thing to be said about pain. Pain isn't ennobling, it's degrading.'

'It's also a warning. Pain prevents you damaging yourself – it tells you something's wrong.'

'You're deliberately missing the point. All right, I'll modify what I said. I intend to avoid self-inflicted pain.'

91

'And you wouldn't inflict any on the other person either?'

'That would be largely her responsibility, wouldn't it? I'm hardly likely to pick a raving neurotic second time around.'

They both realised, simultaneously, that they were heading dangerously close to a row. Michael smiled conciliatorily.

'One day, no doubt, Barbara will sit you down with a very dry Martini and tell you her side of the story. In fact, if I know Babs, that's a treat you won't avoid for long. She's a much better raconteur than me. You'll find her version of our marriage much more entertaining.'

'You make me feel like some sort of double agent,' said Lisa, chastened in the knowledge that his prediction was probably correct.

'You can't help it. Either you'd have to stop cooking for Barbara's house parties, or you stop cooking for me. That would be cutting off your nose to spite your face. And ours. We both need you, Lisa.' He grinned goodnaturedly.

'Are you going to be hiring me again, then?' queried Lisa, casually, her heart leaping.

'Of course. Only next time there won't be so many guests. I enjoy more intimate gatherings. The party wasn't really my type of thing. I only give those bunfights once or twice a year.'

'I hope you don't think I would ever deliberately discuss either of you with the other.'

'Don't worry. As far as Babs is concerned, you won't get a word in edgeways. Just make life easy for both of us, though, and curb your terrifying honesty for once. Don't let on you've seen me again. She's got a one-track mind.'

That much Lisa could believe.

'Now,' said Michael, eyeing the dessert trolley, 'let's

lay off the emotional striptease, shall we, and choose our-
selves a really wicked pudding.'

'Do you eat desserts? Men always seem to go for the
cheese.'

'I'm going to have cheese as well. I'm a growing lad.
Now you know where Jamie gets his famous appetite.'

The rest of the meal was lighthearted and relaxed.
Lingering over several cups of coffee, they were very
nearly the last people to leave the restaurant. Lisa was
amazed at how the time had flown and how many topics
thay had discussed. Going to the powder-room before
they left, she saw that she was looking rather flushed and
excited, a state which she put down to that imprudently
large cherry brandy. The cold night air struck refresh-
ingly against her hot cheeks.

'I've still got your jumper.' The chilly wind reminded
her.

'And I've still got yours,' he smiled. 'It doesn't really
suit me, though. Not my colour.'

'Thank you for the dress, by the way. And the meal. It
was delicious.'

'Restaurants are all very well,' he commented, 'but
they pall a bit when you eat out all the time. That's why
I'm so keen on taking advantage of your good home
cooking.'

'Oh, any time. So far you and Barbara are my only
customers.'

'What you might call an exclusive clientèle. Well, I'd
better get you home. I expect Sarah's waiting up for you
with a mug of piping hot Ovaltine.'

Lisa felt disappointed that the evening was at an end.
She had never enjoyed anyone's company so much. She
reverted momentarily to her well-worn private fantasy of
being cool, mysterious and glamorous. Then she might
stand a chance of holding her own with the likes of

93

Michael Delaney, give him a run for his money. As it was, she ought to be thanking her lucky stars that he had better fish to fry. He stopped the car outside Rochester Terrace.

'Thank you again for a lovely evening,' mumbled Lisa, fiddling with her handbag.

'I'm glad you enjoyed it.'

'Well, then, I'll be saying goodnight.'

'I hoped you would.'

'Would what?'

'Say goodnight. I've never had a braw, bricht, moon-licht one before.'

'What do you mean?'

'I mean, aren't you going to kiss me goodnight?'

In Lisa's experience, this was the point when Douglas, or whoever, grabbed her unceremoniously and started gobbling her face as if he'd missed his dinner. Now here was Michael Delaney, cool as you like, sitting there telling *her* to kiss *him* goodnight!

'Goodnight,' she said brightly, giving him a peck on the cheek.

'Rotten shot. You missed.'

Lisa went crimson. Very quickly, she kissed him on the lips.

'Mmm,' he remarked. 'That's put me in my place. I must change my toothpaste. Or maybe I didn't put on enough Miss Dior.'

'I told you,' croaked Lisa, feeling ridiculous, 'I can only drive a Morris 1100.'

'Then it's time,' he whispered, 'you got your HGV licence.'

She didn't even think to resist his kiss. It was so decep-tively gentle. Deceptive because, gentle or not, she had never before allowed anyone such a leisurely, thorough, exploration of her mouth. Effortlessly, indolently, he took complete possession of it, with a curiosity and can-

94

dour that sent strange throbbing tremors travelling to distant parts of her anatomy. Never had she experienced such an adult, searching kiss, although she realised, heart hammering, that in Michael Delaney's book, this was just kid's stuff. Five minutes of this no doubt had women tearing their clothes off, and his as well. He didn't, however, seem in the least excited, and although he held her close, he kept his hands to himself, as if to prove he could manage perfectly well without them. Unhurriedly, he released her.

'Fresh strawberries,' he said. 'First of the season. Imagine what they would taste like if you added cream and sugar.'

His meaning was uncomfortably clear. Whilst yielding completely to his kiss, she had not dared to participate in it. Transfixed, she had, out of self-preservation, been deliberately passive. She knew she ought to get out of the car now, while the going was good, but her knees felt weak. And it was nothing to do with the cherry brandy.

He lifted her chin so that she met his eyes. No man had ever looked at her quite like that. She began to tremble. He noticed immediately.

'After my jacket this time, are you?' He smiled, breaking the tension. 'Sleep well, Lisa.'

She stumbled up the stairs, praying that Sarah would have gone to bed. Mercifully, she had. 'Sleep well,' he had said, having first ensured that this would prove to be a complete impossibility.

Lisa woke up next day with a hangover, untypically sluggish and bleary-eyed. Alcohol was not so much the culprit as the way she'd tossed and turned all night, trying unsuccessfully to obliterate that kiss from her consciousness. It had awakened something almost distressing deep inside her, something which would have been best left dormant. She tried to find a polite word for it, but there wasn't one. She wanted, there was no getting round it, an awful lot more from him than just one kiss. And infuriatingly, the best she could currently look forward to was catering for those 'more intimate gatherings' he had referred to, at which, no doubt, one of the guests — if not the only guest — would be retained overnight.

There she would be, Lisa Campbell, neat in her cotton dress and mobcap, serving up aphrodisiac *dîners-à-deux*, tactfully clearing off after the coffee. Terrific. Meanwhile, Michael was probably, at this very moment, contemplating more stimulating female company, having found his rendezvous the night before delightfully refreshing, such a nice change to be kissing a simple-minded ingénue whilst recharging his batteries for more strenuous encounters elsewhere . . .

'How did it go?' asked Sarah archly, over breakfast.

'The food was delicious.'

'And?'

'And nothing. I told you.'

'You mean you blew it. Trust you.'

'You have a mind like a sewer.'

'Charming. Be like that, then. I wasn't expecting you to tell me anything anyway,' Sarah sniffed reproachfully.

'I'm sorry, Sarah, that was rude of me. He took me out to dinner, we talked about everything under the sun, and he brought me home. If you must know, he wants me to cook for him again. Small gatherings, he said. Him and one lady friend, most likely. He's bored by restaurants, which is understandable.'

'You mean he didn't even kiss you goodnight?' Sarah looked disbelieving. Lisa hated lying.

'Well, yes, of course he did. Just a friendly kiss, you know.'

'No, I don't know. He doesn't seem the type to give friendly kisses to me. I felt bad after you'd gone, being in,

I mean. I knew you'd be too embarrassed to ask him up with me here.' Sarah sounded so hapless, so apologetic, that Lisa quite forgave her her previous belligerence.

'I wasn't going to ask him up anyway. Honestly, Sarah. Let's face it, I'm not exactly in his league, am I?'

'Hardly,' conceded Sarah frankly, 'but that must be what turns him on. Why don't you make the most of it? It's got to happen one of these days, Lisa, and it might as well be with someone who knows what he's doing. The first time is terribly important, you know.'

Sarah's face was so open and sincere that Lisa burst out laughing and gave her a quick hug.

'When I'm ready, you can hand-pick someone for me,' she teased. 'I'm just not ready yet.'

'It's not all up to you, though, is it?' pointed out Sarah sagely. '*He'll* decide for you. Take it from me. The way I see it, he finds you a bit of a challenge, you're not his usual type. So, he might go for a softly-softly approach at first, but when it comes to the crunch he won't take no for an answer. Just don't say I didn't warn you.'

And, with a new respect in her eyes, Sarah wisely let the subject drop.

Chapter Six

This conversation did nothing to improve Lisa's peace of mind, and she was glad of the distractions of a busy programme at College and another firm booking from the Bentleys. Howard had telephoned her to ask her to come to Lynford Bassett for a whole weekend. Not a house-party, he explained, just general catering for Saturday and Sunday. They still hadn't managed to replace the much-maligned Mrs Duckett. It was agreed that Lisa would travel down with them by car on the Friday night, returning the same way on Sunday evening.

Lisa told herself it was pathetic to keep rushing for the telephone every time it rang, like a lovesick teenager. Apart from Howard, every caller was, as usual, for Sarah – her agent, her hairdresser, her innumerable cronies, and, inevitably, Richard. Was she imagining it, or did Richard speak to her less dismissively these days? Habitually, he barked out long-winded messages and rang off abruptly. Of late, however, he tended to engage in a bit of polite small-talk first, and treat her to rather husky goodbyes. Lisa recoiled from any notion that he might have picked anything up from Michael, who, whatever his other vices, didn't seem the sort to kiss and tell. More likely Sarah had been gossiping, and between them they were busy jumping to conclusions. Which would be all very well, if only their conclusions weren't likely to prove so miserably wrong.

And so the days passed without a word from Michael. It was not in Lisa's nature to moon and mope; she just became increasingly defiant. Next time he expected her to drop everything and come running, she resolved to be otherwise engaged.

On the appointed Friday, the Bentleys' Mercedes drew up outside Rochester Terrace at six o' clock as arranged. Howard hooted and Lisa hurried downstairs, her overnight case in her hand, joining James and Brigitta in the back seat. James was fiddling morosely with a Rubik cube. There was a bit of an atmosphere in the car, Lisa thought.

'I didn't get a chance to ring you about the menus,' Barbara greeted her languidly, 'but I've ordered simply stacks of food and you can do whatever you like with it.'

'Oh good,' beamed Lisa, trying to sound enthusiastic.

'Saturday lunch,' continued Barbara, 'I've got a bridge party. We're invited out that evening, so you can please yourself. Then half a dozen for Sunday lunch again. Perhaps you could knock up a few quiches or something to bring back to London. You should have plenty of time. Howard, can we please have the heater on? I'm frozen stiff.'

A deathly silence followed.

'How are the English classes going, Brigitta?' asked Lisa sociably, unable to face two hours of this ominous hush.

'Well, thank you. We read *The Mill on the Floss*.' Lisa had a vague recollection of neglecting this worthy novel during her mis-spent schooldays.

'That sounds interesting.'

'It's boring,' volunteered James precociously. 'I read the first page.'

'Be polite, Jamie,' cut in Howard, robot-fashion. Barbara appeared to have dozed off, her head slumped to one side. Brigitta had assumed an expression of Teutonic disdain.

'Can we have chips?' asked Jamie, going straight to the point. 'You promised.'

'I expect so. But I didn't promise. I said I'd see what I could do. What other food do you like?'

'Chinese,' replied Jamie promptly, 'from the takeaway. And McDonalds.''

Howard coughed sheepishly. 'Come back, Mrs Duckett, all is forgiven,' he quipped, with uneasy heartiness.

'Last night,' continued Jamie relentlessly, 'we had Kentucky Fried Chicken. Mine was cold.'

Lisa suppressed a giggle. Luckily for Jamie, his mother was asleep.

'Brigitta says English food is rubbish,' Jamie informed Lisa. 'She doesn't even like fish fingers.' He looked at Brigitta witheringly. The aupair sat stonily, refusing to take the bait.

'Once Brigitta made *Linsensuppe mit noodles*,' elaborated Jamie. He made a face and a rude noise.

'*James*,' cut in Howard warningly, as if on autospeak.

'If we have any more nonsense out of *you*,' said Lisa crisply, 'there will definitely be no chips.'

Jamie gave her a seraphic smile and behaved impeccably for the rest of the journey.

Lisa set to as soon as they arrived, realising that everyone must be hungry, and found that Brigitta could provide quite docile unskilled labour if suitably directed. Within an hour she was serving up eggs mayonnaise, spaghetti napoletana and green salad, with fruit and cheese to follow. She got the impression, as the five of them sat round the kitchen table together, that such cosy

100

family gatherings were the exception rather than the rule. Howard and Barbara, it transpired, invariably ate out, while Brigitta and Jamie munched silently in front of the television.

Gratifyingly, however, the atmosphere improved in the glow of this untypically wholesome and well-balanced supper. Howard particularly, jaded by expense-account eating, enjoyed his meal with obvious relish. Barbara didn't eat much, and had more than her fair share of the wine, but she seemed even-tempered enough, displaying a vacuous, Valium-induced calm that was infinitely preferable to her usual staccato acidity.

Howard, it turned out, had some distant Scottish ancestry on his mother's side, and he used this as a basis to discuss the land of his forefathers with Lisa, who humoured him appropriately, glad to keep the conversation running along safe channels. Jamie was demonstrating immaculate table manners, obviously busy earning his entitlement to chips next day. Brigitta was engrossed in her food.

'Time for your bath, young man,' said Howard, as Lisa stood up to make coffee.

'Goodnight, Howard. Goodnight, Barbara. Goodnight, Lisa,' parroted Jamie. '*Gute Nacht*, Brigitta.' Imperceptibly, he managed to invest these irreproachable courtesies with a certain subtle irony.

'Goodnight, Jamie darling,' murmured Barbara, almost sadly, giving him an untypically restrained embrace which, for a change, he returned, suddenly childlike. 'I'll come in and tuck you up later.'

When she wasn't acting the world-weary vamp, thought Lisa, Barbara could look positively vulnerable. Her eyes were strangely hungry as she hugged her son and watched him scamper off.

'Thank you, Lisa dear,' she announced, unexpectedly

101

brisk again. 'We all enjoyed that very much. Brigitta will show you your room. Howard?'

Howard, obeying some unspoken command, trotted after Barbara into the living-room. By the time Lisa took in their coffee, they had both already fallen prey to the soporific effects of the television. Lisa didn't like to wake them, so she left the tray and crept out. Brigitta, having done her share in the kitchen, was putting on her outdoor garb.

'I meet my friend Heide in the village,' she explained. 'You wish also to come?' The invitation was half-hearted. Lisa suspected that some foursome was probably in view.

'That's very kind of you, but no,' she declined firmly. 'Mrs Bentley's asleep in there, so I'd better see that Jamie gets to bed. Which is my room?'

'Go to the top of the stairs and it is first to the left,' indicated Brigitta. 'Goodnight,' and she made a speedy exit, clicking the front door quietly behind her.

While the dishwasher grunted and groaned over its labours, Lisa took stock of the contents of the fridge. True to her word, Barbara had ordered prodigious quantities of food. There would be plenty of scope for devising a suitable menu for the bridge party tomorrow. Lisa was weary. She had had a strenuous day mastering strudel pastry. She would tuck up Jamie on Barbara's behalf and then turn in early herself.

Climbing the stairs, she spotted a door marked 'James's Room. Keep Out'. She knocked tentatively. No answer. She peeped inside. No Jamie. He must still be in the bath. Yes, loud splashing and gurgling noises were emanating from the room at the end of the passage. Leaving him to it for a while, Lisa located her own bedroom. Although small, it was tastefully furnished and expensively decorated, in keeping with the rest of the house. Howard had already brought her case up for her. Sleepily, she unpacked her few things, changed into her dressing gown, and gathered up her spongebag and towel. Yawning, she checked on Jamie again, but his room was still empty. She tapped sternly on the bathroom door.

'Jamie, you've had long enough in there,' she called. 'I'm waiting to use the bathroom. Hurry up and get dry now.'

Silence. No splashing or gurgling even. 'Jamie, did you hear me?' repeated Lisa, trying to sound cross. The quietness was ominous. 'Jamie, are you all right in there?' She persisted, impatient now. This was ridiculous, she wasn't going to be kept waiting by a seven-year-old. She would go in and turf him out. After all, he was only a child.

The door wasn't locked. Entering, she gasped. Jamie was lying face up in the bath, immobile under eighteen inches of water.

'Jamie!' she shrieked, grabbing hold of him and lifting him bodily out of the bath, thinking desperately about artificial respiration. He was a dead weight, amazingly heavy for his size and build. She had him face down on the bath mat in seconds, and was kneeling astride the helpless body and preparing to drive the water from its lungs, when the little shoulders started shaking uncontrollably. Unable to keep his deathly countenance a moment longer, Jamie was chortling away in the throes of some private, diabolical mirth.

'James!' shouted Lisa as he rolled around in glee, quite unselfconsciously. 'Don't you ever *dare* give me a fright like that again!' She threw a towel around him and started rubbing him dry, laughing despite her angry relief. Only then did she notice a miniature model of a shark, with singularly lifelike teeth, floating in the bath. How appropriate, she thought. A plastic duck would be no match for a child like this.

'I suppose you think that was very clever,' she continued to scold him, remembering what Brigitta had told her about the caterpillar in Mrs Duckett's bed. 'That was a very cruel joke to play. You deserve a good hiding.'

'Don't tell Dad on me,' pleaded Jamie, still splitting his sides, 'or he'll give me one.'

'I daresay if I *were* to tell on him,' threatened Lisa, marching him into his bedroom and pulling on his pyjamas, 'he wouldn't take you to the football tomorrow.'

'Cricket,' corrected Jamie. 'If you promise not to,' he negotiated, 'I'll ask him if you can come too. I wouldn't mind *you* coming with us.' The implication, clearly, was that previous Saturday companions had not been so welcome.

'I think your daddy would prefer to have you all to himself,' responded Lisa, colouring slightly at this mention of Michael, 'though I can't imagine why, given what a naughty little boy you are.'

She tucked the covers firmly round him, wondering whether she ought to kiss him goodnight. She had no experience of surrogate motherhood. He solved her problem for her by putting his arms round her neck and planting a damp kiss on her cheek.

'Goodnight, Lisa,' said James, yawning unceremoniously before curling himself up into a little ball and falling instantly asleep.

Uncertain of the morning routine chez Bentley, Lisa took her cue from Jamie, who, first up, was already devouring a bowl of breakfast cereal by the time she got downstairs.

'Barbara has grapefruit and coffee and Howard has toast and peanut butter,' he informed her. 'Brigitta has ham and eggs.'

104

'Would you like some eggs too?' queried Lisa. Jamie beamed. This was luxury.

'Yes please. Scrambled.'

Lisa made scrambled eggs for herself and Jamie, and, taking pity on a heavy-eyed Brigitta, made her breakfast for her as well. On Brigitta's advice, she took the Bentleys theirs in bed, nervously tapping and waiting before entering. Howard was sitting up, blinking, in his striped pyjamas on one side of the king-size bed while Barbara languished sleepily on the other. There was a wide strip of no-man's-land between them.

Returning to the kitchen, Lisa saw that Jamie had already taken up a vantage point in the front room, from which he could anticipate his father's arrival. The thought of seeing Michael again, especially on Barbara's territory, filled her with apprehension. While Brigitta went to wash and dress, Lisa devised the lunch menu, deciding on mushroom vol-au-vents, chicken Kiev, and chocolate mousse. She was very proud of her flaky pastry, scorning the ready-made variety, and decided to get started right away, to give it ample time to rest and chill between stages. She didn't hear the doorbell ring, because Jamie had darted to let Michael in before he had a chance to press it. The kitchen door was open. Looking up, she saw Michael lift Jamie high into the air before setting him down and ruffling his hair. The disparity in their respective sizes made Michael seem even bigger than usual.

'How goes it, son?' he asked Jamie casually.

'Okay, thanks, Dad,' replied Jamie, man to man, controlling any obvious display of excitement. Father and son both caught her eye at once. Flustered, she drew a floury hand across her brow.

'Good morning, Lisa,' Michael greeted her blandly. 'At it already, I see.'

'Good morning, Mr Delaney,' replied Lisa with deliberate correctness. 'Mrs Bentley's having some friends in for lunch.'

'How super,' he commented dryly. 'Jamie, run up and tell your mother I'm here.' Jamie disappeared up the stairs. Michael walked into the kitchen and smoothed the flour from her forehead with provocative fingers. Neither of them spoke. Lisa, who had intended to be pointedly formal and distant with him, found all her resolve crumbling the moment he touched her. She attacked her pastry with anything but a light touch.

'You're a bit tense this morning, aren't you?' he remarked in a puzzled tone. 'Is the atmosphere here getting to you already? Or are you just embarrassed at me being here?'

'I suppose so, a bit,' she found herself admitting. 'It makes me feel like pig in the middle.'

'I'm sorry I didn't ring you,' he continued, reading her thoughts. 'It must have seemed like I'd forgotten you. I hadn't.'

How mortifying, thought Lisa, that he should so easily have detected her quite unjustified pique at his prolonged silence.

'I wasn't expecting to hear from you,' she protested airily. 'In any case, I've been up to my eyes in work, and ...' But to save her further duplicity Jamie skipped in, to be followed, disconcertingly, by Barbara, fragile in a cream chiffon wrap. Despite her early morning pallor, or perhaps because of it, her ethereal beauty was more striking and poignant than ever. Lisa crossed to the sink and started wiping and slicing mushrooms, pointedly keeping her back to them.

'What's happening today then, Babs?' she heard Michael ask with curt politeness.

'Howard and I are invited to Steve Wainwright's this

106

evening, so we won't be around when you get back. Lisa will let you in. Don't bring him back too late, it's time he had an early night.' Her voice had a certain hostile coquetry. 'You look pretty tired yourself,' she added, accusingly. The air was heavy with innuendo.

'I got up very early to drive down here,' explained Michael impassively. 'Couldn't get away last night. Put your anorak on then, Jamie.'

Lisa turned round to catch Barbara giving her ex-husband an inflammatory look, midway between naked desire and outright hatred.

''Bye, Lisa. See you, Babs,' said Michael, unperturbed. Jamie was already out of the house and clambering into the car. The door slammed. Barbara had an air of crumpled defiance. Ignoring Lisa, she went back upstairs.

The rest of the morning passed busily. Howard went off for a day's golf, giving Barbara a lift into the village on his way. Brigitta wielded a hoover and duster around the house in a desultory fashion. She would clearly have preferred to sit idly gossiping, but Lisa, furiously absorbed in her own work, found herself supervising Brigitta sternly. She seemed a lazy sort of girl to her and the whole place, dusty from neglect, was badly in need of a good going over before the guests arrived at noon. Realising that Lisa was not a willing partner in crime, Brigitta got on with her duties, and, to her credit, the cottage displayed a Germanic spotlessness by the time Lisa went to set the table.

Barbara returned from the village, her colour much improved by her walk, looking uncharacteristically county in brogues and a silk headsquare. After changing into a white trouser suit, which showed off her slim figure to great advantage, she was in fine fettle by the time her guests arrived, three rather shrill upper-class ladies who, disappointingly for Lisa, all seemed to be trying to out-rival each other in the diet stakes.

Each course was pecked at and toyed with in the most infuriating manner, although they managed, nonetheless, to knock back three bottles of chilled hock between them. The meal was over within an hour, and by the time Lisa took in their coffee, they were already immersed in their bridge. No-one even acknowledged her, let alone commented on the meal, and it offended Lisa's natural good sense and thriftiness to see all that wasted food ending up in the bin. There had been nothing wrong with it, Brigitta had demolished hers with gusto.

She was determined, however, not to show her chagrin, ridiculing herself privately for her newly discovered tendency to indulge in outraged artistic temperament. After relieving her frustrations somewhat by 'knocking up a few quiches' as requested – a mere couple of hours' routine work – she was forced to resign herself to an afternoon and evening of unmitigated boredom. Lisa had no desire to foist herself on Brigitta, despite her colleague's limp invitation to accompany her and a friend to the cinema that afternoon. Peeved and listless, she sprawled disconsolately on her bed, idly perusing the book on French regional cookery she had brought along with her. One thing about the French, she reflected morosely, was that they really seemed to appreciate their food. Unlike some people she could mention . . .

She didn't know what to make of Barbara, even in the light of the little Michael had told her. Undoubtedly, she was a very complex sort of person. She obviously still had some kind of love-hate thing going with Michael, worshipped her child in a sentimental fashion, and abused her well-meaning and long-suffering husband. She sparkled, sulked or spat, according to her mood. She drank too much and ate too little. She was extraordinarily beautiful.

108

Beautiful enough to command, and get, everything she could possibly want. And clearly, despite all that, she was desperately unhappy.

Lisa must have dozed off, and woke, startled, to find Barbara leaning over her bed.

'I'm so sorry, Mrs Bentley,' she muttered, confused, looking at her watch. 'Were you wanting some more coffee?'

Barbara sat down sociably on the bed. Her eyes were unnaturally bright.

'No, no, they've left, don't worry. Are you quite well?'

'Oh yes, absolutely. I must have fallen asleep, I –'

'Don't apologise. I expect you were bored stiff, up here all on your own. You could have gone out with Brigitta, you know.' Her tone was surprisingly friendly, her mood mellow. There was a faint hint of brandy lurking behind her perfume. But she didn't appear in the least drunk, thank goodness.

'As it is,' she continued, 'I'm afraid you'll have to hang around now until Michael and James get home, and then, of course, it's Brigitta's night off and James can't be left on his own. Still, we do expect to make it worth your while.'

Lisa jumped up. 'Well, I'd better get on and clear the coffee cups,' she said briskly. Barbara caught hold of her arm and pressed her back into a sitting position.

'Don't go,' she said, almost plaintively. 'Cigarette?' She proffered a gold cigarette case. Lisa didn't smoke, although she had the odd puff when wishing to appear sophisticated. Instinctively recognising Barbara's plea for company, she took one and accepted a light.

'Tell me, what do you think of James?' asked Barbara. echoing the question Michael had once asked, and drawing deeply on her cigarette while Lisa held hers self-consciously between two inexpert fingers.

'He's very grown up for his age,' ventured Lisa uncertainly.

'Do you think so? I've no-one to compare him with, really. He's a good-looking child, isn't he?'

This had the air of a trick question, given that Jamie so closely resembled his father.

'Very,' agreed Lisa. 'He's got your ... er, nose.'

'Of course he hasn't,' snapped Barbara testily. 'He doesn't take after me at all. Trust those damn Delaney genes to get the upper hand! Still, I suppose I shouldn't complain, in view of his father's obvious ... attractiveness.' She flung Lisa a hard, rather penetrating look. 'Just as long as he doesn't inherit his perfectly putrid character.'

Lisa was horrified. She couldn't possibly participate in such a conversation. It was all very well if Barbara wanted to vent her feelings in front of a close friend or relative, but it was quite inappropriate for her to be confiding in the temporary cook. Lisa shifted uncomfortably on the bed, but couldn't cut Barbara short without seeming rude, or looking as if she were leaping to Michael's defence.

'I suppose,' continued Barbara, 'you can't wait to get married.'

'No indeed,' protested Lisa. 'I – '

'Take my tip,' went on Barbara, interrupting her. 'Don't. I should know. I've tried it twice. I didn't even have the wit to learn my lesson the first time.'

'Mrs Bentley, I really think – '

'Am I embarrassing you?' smiled Barbara sweetly. 'No need. If I don't tell you my troubles, somebody else soon will. Brigitta, for example, within the limits of her vocabulary, of course. And her obvious bias towards 'Mistair Delanee'. Have you seen the way she ogles him? Poor bitch doesn't stand a chance. He loathes big

110

women. You're more the shape he goes for.' She eyed Lisa candidly. 'How exactly did you come to do that party for him?'

'Through my flatmate,' explained Lisa, adding hastily, fearing misconstruction, 'her boyfriend is a photographer too, and he knew Mr Delaney needed help.'

'You did very well. He'll probably find himself needing help again. Beware, my child. Don't have anything to do with him unless you have some kind of emotional death-wish.'

Lisa couldn't help herself. She went as red as her hair. Barbara's lip curled in amusement as she blew out a long luxurious trail of smoke.

'Don't tell me you've already got a crush on him? How charming. And how wonderful for his over-inflated ego. He already considers himself irresistible. Admittedly, in some ways he is. If you could spend absolutely all your time in bed with him, he'd be extremely good company. Unfortunately, outside the jolly old boudoir, he's a perfect bastard.'

Lisa was beginning to realise that Barbara was, despite the lack of any overt symptons, under the influence of the wine and brandy she had consumed. If these indescretions continued, she would probably be mortified once she was sober.

'Mrs Bentley, I don't think it's my place to − ' But Barbara cut her short. 'Unlike Howard,' she went on. 'With him, the problem's the other way round. Pity one can't have two husbands. One as a sort of male concubine, purely for pleasure, and the other to worry about you, look after you, and take care of all the bills.'

Barbara was in full flow now. Lisa accepted the futility of trying to escape. She sat, trying not to listen. An impossible resolution, of course, given the morbid fascination of the subject under discussion.

'When I first got married,' reminisced Barbara, 'I was only about your age. I'd led a very sheltered life, I was terribly trusting. Michael literally swept me off my feet. He has a very direct approach. Never confuse directness with honesty, Lisa, it's not the same thing at all. For Michael, a woman has only one function in life. He's quite incapable of love himself and despises it in others. Three years of hell, I had with him. Do you know, while I was giving birth to James he was somewhere in bloody South America. Would you believe, he didn't even see his son till he was nearly three weeks old.' There was a mounting crescendo of self-pity in her voice. 'Of course, he's imbued with good old working-class morality – the man supports the family and amuses himself as he pleases, while the wife sits faithfully at home with the kids. Talk about the double standard! Don't ever fall for it, Lisa dear, what's sauce for the gander is quite definitely sauce for the goose. Except when the gander happens to be Howard. He's a very sweet man, don't you agree?'

'Y – yes,' mumbled Lisa. 'Very nice.'

'Just the word I was looking for, Lisa. Nice. Terribly, terribly nice.' The word was saturated with boredom. 'No, the only worthwhile relic of my ventures into matrimony is James. I adore him, Lisa, truly I do, but it seems I just wasn't cut out for motherhood. Perhaps we'll get on better when he's a bit older. If only I could look at him without seeing Michael written all over him. If only he'd been a girl.'

Lisa saw two gleaming tears suspended in the pale blue eyes, and without pausing to think, put her arm round Barbara's shoulders. She half expected a rebuff, it had been rather a forward gesture, but instead Barbara leaned her head against her and sobbed silently. The tears were genuine, and the lack of sound, the muteness of her weeping, was strangely pathetic. Lisa was uncharacteristically

112

lost for words. There was, quite simply, no comfort she could offer. Barbara's life, despite its superficial compensations, was a mess.

After some minutes, Barbara wiped her eyes on the bedcover and pulled herself together with an effort.

'How beastly for you,' she observed, her voice suddenly dry, 'having to play agony aunt. I shall have to ask Howard to pay you a bonus. Sorry, I shoudn't have said that.' The apology had an air of challenge. Lisa rose to it.

'I'm flattered you should trust me, Mrs Bentley. I wish I could help more than just by listening.'

'You will come again, won't you?' demanded Barbara. 'You won't pretend you're busy next time?'

Lisa felt horribly compromised. Financially, her arrangement with the Bentleys was a godsend. Morally, and culinarily, it was totally unsatisfactory.

'To be perfectly honest with you,' she confessed bravely, 'I don't feel I earn my fee. Look at lunch, for example. You didn't need me at all, sandwiches would have done as well. No-one was hungry.'

'Oh, Lisa,' soothed Barbara, instantly charming again and fully in control. 'Everyone mentioned how delectable the food was. It was just far, far too much. Why, I had more appetite than I've had for simply ages. How dreadfully rude of us not to compliment you. I'm afraid we take our bridge far too seriously. Do you know, I won £12 today?'

Lisa was amazed at the ingenuous delight in Barbara's voice. Though she'd never had to earn her living, never been short of money – or perhaps because of this – bridge winnings gave her a certain self-esteem.

'Besides,' Barbara reassured her, 'today wasn't typical. Women never eat much, specially when they're on their own. Sunday lunch will be more worthwhile, from your point of view. I mean, look at how much Howard and Jamie eat. I don't know where Jamie puts it all.' She rose, astonishingly cheerful in view of her recent lapse into misery. Perhaps she was a manic-depressive, thought Lisa. In any event, she now seemed to take it for granted that Lisa had guaranteed her continuing availability.

'I must have a bath and get changed,' she announced brightly. 'We're likely to be back from Steve's very late, so don't wait up. I doubt if you'll see Brigitta much before midnight – you won't need three guesses what *she* gets up to in the village. Michael usually brings James back around eight or so. They'll already have eaten. Do help yourself to whatever you want. Howard will show you how to use the video.'

She gave Lisa a rather patronising peck on the cheek.

'You're a real treasure, Lisa,' she cooed, and glided off.

Lisa found snippets of their strange conversation drifting back to her unbidden throughout the rest of the afternoon. As Michael had predicted, Barbara's version of their marriage was different from his, or perhaps not so different after all. He was incapable of love, she had said. She had languished in the labour ward while he got himself shot at thousands of miles away. Outside the bedroom he was a perfect bastard. There wasn't so much a conflict of fact, she surmised, as a difference of slant, a rift in interpretation. She remembered Michael's treatise about love being like a loaded gun. He too, by his own account, had suffered, had loved, had lost. What man could possibly have coped with Barbara? What woman could possibly have coped with Michael? Neither of them, she concluded, should ever have got married in the first place, let alone to each other. A clean break might have allowed the bullet wounds to heal. But there could be no clean break, not with Jamie as a living reminder of what there had once been between them.

114

On balance, she concluded, her sympathies lay with Barbara — disillusioned, vulnerable and neurotic — rather than with her tough, resilient, self-sufficient ex-husband. But, inevitably, it was Jamie who commanded her true allegiance.

Howard returned soon after this interview, ruddy from his day on the golf course. He greeted Lisa cordially, tutored her in the use of the televison, hi-fi and video, told her to feel free to help herself to any of his books, and then shot off upstairs to change.

Judging by the books and records he possessed, Howard was a regular culture-vulture, to the extent of being quite dauntingly highbrow. Only his video library revealed, rather endearingly, a taste for westerns, ancient gangster films, and Carry On comedies. There was little evidence of Barbara's tastes in anything much. Clothes, bridge, and a hectic social life were presumably her main interests. Lisa wondered what she had ever found in common with Howard. Or with Michael, for that matter. But of course, the answers to both those questions had been provided, quite explicitly, by Barbara herself.

The Bentleys set off for Steve Wainwright's at seven-thirty, Barbara looking animated, radiant, and perfectly ravishing in a low-cut black dress. As the Mercedes disappeared down the driveway, Lisa decided to make herself a snack supper of some sort. Barbara had said Michael and Jamie would have eaten already, and it hardly seemed worth cooking anything much, just for one. She paused, and on impulse started peeling and chipping potatoes, feeling a sudden urge to have this humble treat available for Jamie's return, in case he chould claim to be still hungry — a quite likely eventuality, she suspected. In any case, she might as well cook a few now, for herself, with a couple of eggs. She began heating a large saucepan of oil.

She was just drying some chips in a teatowel before frying them when the doorbell rang. Wiping her hands, she went to let Michael and Jamie in.

'I'm hungry,' was the first thing Jamie said. Michael looked at her sheepishly, and gave a comical shrug of despair.

'We had some hot dogs at the match,' he explained with a boyish grin, 'and a couple of ice creams at the pictures. You don't happen to have a horse handy, do you? We could both eat one.'

A yelp of glee emanated from the kitchen, where Jamie had spotted what was in store. He was already setting the table for three, complete with tomato ketchup and vinegar from the larder.

'Can we have baked beans too?' he demanded. 'Please,' he added, responding to a stern look from Michael.

'Go and wash your hands and face,' barked Michael. Jamie scurried off obediently to the bathroom.

As soon as he was gone, the air began to pulsate. Lisa began lowering chips into the hot fat. They sizzled loudly. She fetched a can of baked beans and opened it, aware that Michael was lounging back in one of the kitchen chairs, watching her.

'Lisa,' he murmured softly, beckoningly. She looked round automatically at the sound of her name, her eyes latching involuntarily on to his. He didn't speak, didn't move. He just looked. Lisa's insides did a somersault. The look was challenging, inquisitive, inviting, suggestive, mocking, all in one. Mercifully, Jamie came bounding back into the room.

'Did you have a nice time today?' Lisa asked him, as she cracked eggs into the pan. Jamie needed no prompting to give a ball by ball account of the cricket until rain stopped play. He then launched into a detailed résumé of the science fiction film which had followed.

Michael watched his prattling son with a wry, amused tolerance. It struck Lisa that he probably found minor sporting fixtures and 'U' certificate films less than riveting entertainment. Not all estranged fathers, she mused, were so punctilious about their duties, especially ones with no lack of more attractive diversions for their limited leisure time. His expression remained slightly guarded, however, as if he were unwilling to reveal the extent of the indulgence and affection he must surely feel.

'That's enough, Jamie,' he broke in, as Jamie began denigrating the love interest between the female astronaut and the captain of the spaceship, in typically precocious manner. Jamie shut up cheerfully, faced with a tempting heap of golden chips. He helped himself liberally to the tomato sauce and readily obeyed Lisa's command to start eating while she cooked some more for herself and Michael. With Jamie busily chomping away, conversation lapsed.

'Would you like a sherry or something?' asked Lisa while they were waiting, desperate to break the tension, but uncertain if it was correct etiquette to make free with the Bentleys' hospitality.

'No, not sherry, thanks. Perhaps I'll take you up on . . . something, later,' smiled Michael. Lisa gulped. She found that she had completely lost her appetite, which was just as well as Jamie was already on the lookout for seconds and made sure that Lisa's helping was not wasted. By the time he had finished his ice cream, while Lisa and Michael drank coffee, it was nearly nine o' clock and Michael ordered him sternly to have his bath and go to bed. At the mention of the word 'bath' Jamie looked uncertainly at Lisa. She pursed her mouth in mock indecision, and then gave him a reassuring wink.

'Night, Dad. Night, Lisa,' he shouted as he raced up the stairs.

'If you're not asleep with the light off by quarter past,' Michael called after him, 'I'll come up there and wallop you.'

Jamie appeared to enjoy the rather heavy-handed treatment Michael dished out. Perhaps he found it re-freshing after the flaccid leniency of Howard and Barbara.

'Aren't you going to go up and tuck him in?' asked Lisa, surprised at Michael's abrupt goodnight and Jamie's acceptance of it.

'Certainly not,' retorted Michael dryly. 'He gets enough slop as it is from his mother.'

'You're very hard,' pouted Lisa, thinking wistfully of the warm little bundle she had put to bed the previous night.

'You've been talking to Barbara,' he observed accurately. 'Yes, I have stopped beating my wife. Let's go and sit somewhere more comfortable.'

'Aren't you leaving?' blustered Lisa.

'What do you think?' he asked coolly, his voice loaded with implication.

'I – I was hoping to have an early night,' she stammered.

'Is that an invitation?' he queried, advancing on her and trapping her against the sink.

She was powerless against his kiss, the newly familiar mouth already instilling in her the beginnings of addiction. Sweeter, more sensuous, even more suggestive than its predecessor, this kiss divested her of strength, will and reason. This time, heedless of her better judgement, she responded. An emotional death-wish, Barbara had called it. She was breathless when he released her.

'I must say you've improved,' he commented. 'Have you been practising?' The mood was broken. Lisa wrenched her arms free.

118

'That wasn't fair,' she hissed. 'You caught me off guard. I think you should leave now, and I'd rather you didn't kiss me again.'

'You'd rather nothing of the sort,' he mocked, hands in pockets, apparently unperturbed. 'But, of course, I will go if you really want me to.'

'I want you to!' exclaimed Lisa, fearful of what might happen if he stayed. She didn't seriously expect him, of course, to comply, but infuriatingly he got out his car keys and jingled them tormentingly.

'Never let it be said I forced myself on a woman.' He smiled, his voice perfectly amiable, his eyes warm, taking in her flushed cheeks, heaving breast, flashing eyes. 'Will you come and cook dinner next Thursday?' he asked politely. 'Just for myself and a friend?'

'I'm not sure,' she prevaricated, miserably aware that he was, in fact, about to leave, and fairly sure that he had called her bluff to prove a point.

'Want to ask Barbara's permission first?'

'All right then,' she capitulated sullenly.

'You bring the food,' he said, letting himself out. 'Nothing too heavy,' he added significantly. And he was gone, leaving Lisa full of gnawing pains and a mixture of relief and regret at what she had escaped.

Chapter Seven

Not only did she have difficulty in getting off to sleep that night, but her belated slumber was broken into in the early hours by the sound of raised voices. Howard and Barbara, having returned from their dinner engagement, were having the mother and father of a row as they mounted the stairs. They continued shouting at each other outside the door, and inside their bedroom. Disconcertingly, she could hear every word. Amazingly, Howard was the more vociferous of the two.

'I don't know why you didn't stay there overnight!' he was yelling. 'I'm fed up playing gooseberry, do you hear?'

'Perhaps I will next time!' fulminated Barbara shrilly. 'I'd be off tomorrow if it wasn't for James!'

Lisa was appalled. What if the child should hear all this?

'Perhaps I might just beat you to it,' bellowed Howard. 'I've had about enough of being made a fool of!'

'Shut up!' shrieked Barbara. 'You'll wake him!' And suddenly both their voices dropped and the bedroom door, still ajar, clicked shut. Lisa was wondering whether she ought to check on Jamie, when she heard a tap on her door and the sound of its opening quietly. It wasn't

Jamie, as she had feared. It was Brigitta. Her eyes were alight with malicious amusement.

'You have heard?' she asked unnecessarily, Lisa being bolt upright in bed and plainly wide awake.

'Is Jamie still asleep?' fretted Lisa in some distress. Brigitta shrugged. 'He has heard worse than this,' she explained. 'That child knows.'

Lisa shook her head, only half-listening as Brigitta, with apparent glee, started filling her in on the more sordid details of Barbara's liaison with Steve Wainwright. He often called on Barbara in London, it seemed, while Jamie was at school and Howard at the office. Plainly these were more than just courtesy visits.

'Mr Wainwright works for the television,' elaborated Brigitta. 'He is recently divorced. I think perhaps Mrs Bentley will become another Mrs Wainwright.' Brigitta seemed positively excited at the prospect of such a scandal. Lisa just felt sorry for Howard, sorry for Jamie, strangely sorry for Barbara too in her pointless, ravenous quest for happiness.

'Please go away, Brigitta,' she said coldly. 'I want to get back to sleep.'

An air of uneasy, rather heavy calm hung over Sunday. The lunch party passed without incident. Lisa was relieved that Steve Wainwright was not invited on this occasion. She was rapidly beginning to find the Bentley ménage quite stifling. She marvelled increasingly at Jamie's sang-froid, his ability to switch off. He sat between Lisa and Brigitta on the way back to London, enjoying the unaccustomed diversion of playing 'I spy' with Lisa. Howard joined in the game rather stiffly, while Barbara filed her nails with a vengeance. Brigitta refused to participate, engrossing herself in a large and shapeless piece of knitting.

Lisa felt a wrench when they dropped her off, fighting

an insane impulse to grab Jamie and make a run for it. She was getting ridiculously emotional about the child. Quite inappropriately, she told herself. He was, without doubt, a little monster.

''Bye, Lisa dear,' purred Barbara. 'We'll be in touch.'

When Lisa got inside, another large cheque safely in her handbag, she made an unscheduled and extravagant phone call to her father, craving the reassuring normality of his voice. He sounded tired, and touchingly glad to hear from her. For two pins, thought Lisa, I'd catch the next train home.

Thursday evening, however, found Lisa very much still in London, grimly pressing the buzzer outside Montpelier Gardens. A husky female voice over the entryphone invited her up. Lisa gave a mental snort. This evening, she would overcharge him outrageously. She did not feel in the least bit like cooking, having spent an energetic day wrestling with yeast doughs.

Michael was not around to greet her. His female companion, however, welcomed her cordially and offered her a drink, which she declined. The girl was about twenty-five, with an American accent. Very laid back, thought Lisa sourly. Literally. Tall, tanned and leggy with high cheekbones and short dark hair, her casual attire betrayed her familiarity with Michael. No recent conquest invited to supper at his flat would arrive wearing faded old jeans and a tee shirt. Though perhaps, reflected Lisa bitchily, if she was a *very* good friend, she would be slipping into the bedroom shortly to change into something more comfortable.

She set about her work ferociously. Michael and his girlfriend remained ensconced in the studio. She could hear them talking and laughing when she went to set the table. 'Nothing too heavy,' he had specified. The mind boggled at what post-prandial gymnastics he had in mind.

122

Spotting some ordinary white candles under the kitchen sink — the sort one keeps for power cuts — she stuck two of them unceremoniously in a couple of egg cups and placed them in the centre of the table with a venomous flourish.

The dessert was a cold one — crème brûlée — and as soon as she had served the veal escalopes, she was planning to leave them to it. The starter was fresh pears with Parma ham. She left it out on the table and shut herself in the kitchen. She would soon hear, by the clanking of knives and forks, when they had started. She stood glaring at the raw escalopes, and began taking it out on the innocent tagliatelle, viciously snapping pieces of it between irritable fingers. It was already nearly eight o' clock. She had hoped to be gone by half-past.

Michael put his head round the door. 'The wine,' he prompted. 'Should it be red or white?'

'White, I expect,' shrugged Lisa. 'You're having veal.'

'Oh, in that case I think a rosé would be rather fun, don't you?' asked Michael breezily, opening the fridge and selecting a couple of chilled bottles. 'Sort of seasonal in this lovely summer weather we're having.' He held the bottles up quizzically. 'What do you think?'

'I'm sure I don't know,' bit back Lisa. 'Why don't you ask your lady friend?'

'I suppose I could' he mused. 'She'll be home in half an hour or so. I could phone her then and ask her opinion. But meanwhile, we'd be getting rather peckish.'

Lisa looked at him blankly. He grinned and uncorked one of the bottles.

'I suggest you put that lot on now,' he remarked, indicating the veal and pasta. 'They can be cooking while we're eating the first course. You don't want to have to jump up and start cooking again.'

'I beg your pardon?'

Masterfully, he took over, heating the sauté pan and bringing the water back to the boil. While she looked on, dumbstruck, he chucked the pasta into the pan and dropped the escalopes into the hot butter. Then he grabbed her hand, sat her down at the table, and poured the wine.

'Cheers,' he said genially, raising his glass.

'W – what's happened to your guest?' faltered Lisa.

'That wasn't my guest,' he explained succinctly. 'Marva's doing some darkroom work for me. And no, I haven't slept with her.'

'I didn't ask you if you had!'

'No, but you were wondering, weren't you? Eat up, it's delicious.'

Her resolve was already melting, like an icicle in a thaw. Reluctantly, she tackled her hors d'oeuvre. It was Michael who cleared the plates away and served the second course.

'Silly me,' he chided himself as he sat down again 'I forgot to light the candles.' He quickly corrected the error and dimmed the lights. Hoist with her own petard, Lisa looked at his mischievous expression over the flickering flame.

'I didn't realise you were such a romantic little soul,' he observed mockingly.

It was hopeless. Unable to keep her face straight any longer, she had to concede defeat. Michael had simply picked up where he had left off after their evening at Leith's. Relaxed, amusing, with his charm nicely honed for the kill, she knew that this time he meant to have things all his own way. The prospect was at the same time frightening and enticing. His magnetism was simply inescapable. Physically, she became more acutely aware of him by the minute, tormented by the tantalising sight, sound and smell of him just inches away from her. He was evidently, however, still out to teach her a lesson because, even sitting next to her on the settee over coffee, he made no move to kiss her, and avoided touching her even accidentally.

By midnight they were still chatting away merrily like old chums, with a surface banter that belied the surging undercurrents. Lisa was becoming quietly desperate as the minutes ticked by. She could not recollect ever having had this problem before. So adept had she become at warding off unwelcome advances that she had never given any thought as to how best to invite welcome ones. It was too late for tactics. She took a deep breath.

'Michael,' she said boldly. 'Will you kiss me?'

'Nope. Not after that brush-off I got last time. If you really want a kiss, you'll have to fix one for yourself.'

'That sounds like a challenge.'

'It was meant to,' responded Michael, giving her a look that sent strange shooting sensations through her arms and legs.

'No Campbell,' she whispered, 'can resist a challenge.'

She kissed him, shyly at first. But he made it impossible for her to stay shy for long. It didn't stop at kissing either, not that she had expected it to, although she could never have imagined herself submitting to, let alone encouraging, the intimacies which followed. There was no doubt whatsoever about where it was all leading. Sarah had been right. Michael certainly knew what he was doing.

'Sure, now?' he murmured in response to her unspoken but clear invitation, before lifting her up in his arms and heading for the bedroom. Lisa nodded, too full of desire to speak. Her impulsive streak had got the better of her, she knew that. But, helpless as a feather in a hurricane, she also knew that this was about to be the biggest, bravest adventure of her life, and one she had gone into with her eyes wide open. If he'd set about seducing her

125

conventionally, of course, she would have felt bound to resist. Clever enough to know it, he had planned his strategy accordingly.

Act in haste, repent at leisure, thought Lisa hazily. This was madness, but she felt no fear, just impatience. Her present pitch of excitement had been built up to languorously, teasingly. He had not tried to rush her. She had had ample opportunity to say 'Stop', and yet no opportunity at all.

They were on the threshold of the bedroom when the entryphone buzzed.

'Ignore it,' said Michael. He laid her on the bed and began removing such items of clothing as were left to her. It buzzed again, long and loud this time. Michael swore under his breath, sensing Lisa's sudden tension.

'I said, ignore it,' he repeated soothingly. Clearly whoever it was had a finger on the bell because a long, continuous buzz ensued.

'You've got to answer it,' wailed Lisa miserably, coming down from her high with a thump. 'It might be important.'

He kissed her briefly. 'Stay right there,' he told her. 'Whoever it is, I'll get rid of her. I mean him.' He grimaced at his own faux pas. Lisa started coming to her senses rather rapidly, like a person waking up from an anaesthetic. She looked at her panties, lying next to Michael's shirt on the floor. What had she nearly done? She could hear his voice clearly in the next room.

'Oh, my God,' he was saying, 'you'd better come up.'

He returned quickly, bringing various discarded garments with him.

'Change of plan,' he said dryly, handing them to her. 'Howard's on the doorstep. There's been some almighty row or other. He says he's left Barbara. He's in a hell of a state.'

126

He turned his back as he bent down to pick up his shirt. Only then did she notice the scars Jamie had once referred to — jagged, puckered lines running from his right shoulder blade down his side and beyond the hip bone. Old scars, obviously, but still bearing witness to a serious and probably very painful injury, marring the firm, sinewy flesh. She fought the urge to trace the line of the wound with her fingers. He thrust muscular arms back into shirt sleeves and began buttoning his cuffs. Lisa swallowed hard. Had that powerful body really been about to take possession of hers? She started scrambling into her clothes.

'Shall I, er — stay in here?' she asked, her face hot with colour.

'It's up to you. I wouldn't worry about what Howard thinks. He's unshockable. He'd hardly have married Barbara if he wasn't. I'd rather you came in, actually. I hate hole-in-the-corner stuff.'

There was a knock at the front door and Michael went to answer it, tucking in his shirt as he did so, while Lisa tried hastily to tidy her hair.

'Sorry, old man,' Howard was muttering as she joined them in the living room. 'Sorry to spring myself on you like this — oh ... good evening, Lisa.' Miraculously, he didn't seem overly surprised to see her. Given her own, and Michael's, tousled appearance and the lateness of the hour, any assumptions he might make were likely to be correct — or very nearly.

Michael was pouring Howard a large Scotch. Howard was shaking. Lisa felt distinctly *de trop*. Whatever he needed to tell Michael was private, after all.

'I think I'll just phone for a taxi,' she mumbled.

'Not yet,' said Michael. 'Howard, Lisa's being delicate. You don't mind her being here, do you?'

'But I, er . . .' broke in Lisa, horribly embarrassed on Howard's behalf.

Howard, however, gave her a weak smile and said reassuringly, 'Please don't leave on my account, Lisa. What I'm about to say won't be private for very much longer, in any case.'

He took a slug of whisky, his face ravaged with pain. Michael remained standing, his expression inscrutable. Lisa sat down next to Howard and put her hand on his arm in a gesture of sympathy. He flung her a grateful look, his eyes misty behind the hornrimmed glasses.

'I've left her,' he began. 'She wasn't expecting me back tonight, I had a business meeting in Manchester and I was planning to stay over. But I got through earlier than expected so I caught the last shuttle home. I tried ringing to tell her but the line was engaged.'

'When I got in, the house was dark. I crept upstairs very quietly, looked in on James as usual, and got undressed in the bathroom so as not to wake her, you know. There I am, tiptoeing into the bedroom in pyjamas and bare feet, quiet as a mouse, and – well, you can guess what I found.' His tone was defeated rather than angry.

'I could have forgiven the thing itself, I suppose. I mean, I knew she and Wainwright were having a fling, but I told myself, "He's not the first and he won't be the last." You know how she is, Mike. But then the pair of them started laying into me as if *I* was the one in the wrong. Barbara calls me a peeping Tom, would you believe, and Wainwright, cool as you please, invites me to take a seat and watch if I want to, I might pick up a few tips! I nearly went for him. He would have slaughtered me, of course, but I was quite beside myself, as you can imagine. Barbara was enjoying it, practically licking her lips at the thought of the two of us fighting over her.

'Then I remembered Jamie asleep across the passage.

Thank God, I managed to keep control. I told her I was leaving and wouldn't be back. She said that was fine by her, she was sick of the sight of me anyway, and Wainwright just laughed. The worrying thing about it, Mike, is that Barbara wasn't quite ... er ... herself. Not just booze this time either, I know the signs too well by now. I think Wainwright's got her on something worse.'

'Drugs,' said Michael crisply. 'I've been suspecting it for some weeks.'

Lisa was open-mouthed. Howard's head hung down, defeated.

'You mean — hard drugs?' gasped Lisa, horrified.

'I've heard that Wainwright's set go in for sniffing,' admitted Howard awkwardly.

'What, glue?'

'Cocaine, Lisa,' rapped Michael, impatiently.

'I'm seeing my solicitor in the morning,' went on Howard woodenly. 'This isn't as sudden as it may look, it's just the straw that's finally broken my back. I can't begin to tell you some of the other things, I'd be too ashamed.'

Lisa could feel his whole body vibrating. She looked at Michael desperately, sensing that Howard was going to break down any moment. As if by telepathy, Michael tactfully left the room. Relieved, Howard leant against Lisa, totally shattered, and, her arm around his shoulders, she comforted him as silent, strangled sobs wracked his body.

After several minutes Michael returned. 'I've made up the divan for you in the spare room, Howard. I'll come to your solicitors with you tomorrow, before I go to see my own.'

'Of course,' nodded Howard. 'Jamie. You realise, Mike, there was nothing I could do? I'd have taken him like a shot, I'm really fond of the little chap and I hated leaving him with Wainwright there. But she'd never have let him go voluntarily, and of course I've absolutely no chance of getting custody.'

'No,' said Michael grimly. 'But I have. Get your things, Lisa. I'll drive you home.'

Michael hardly said a word to her in the car going home. Understandably, she thought, he was preoccupied, his face set into hard lines of determination.

'Do you think he really means it?' she asked tentatively.

'You don't know Howard,' he replied shortly. 'Types like him are like dormant volcanoes. He's put up, I'd guess, with more than anyone can imagine. It's time he got out before she turns him into a complete eunuch. He's got a good relationship with his ex-wife and grown-up daughters. They know all about Barbara. They'll rally round. If I spot him weakening, I'll step in.'

He stopped the car. The intimacy had fled, his eyes were far away. He gave her a brief, abstracted kiss.

'I'm going to be busy over the next few days, Lisa,' he began.

'Of course,' she mumbled, getting out of the car hastily. 'Goodnight, Michael.'

It was dark in the flat. Sarah was still out. Lisa sat in the kitchen for a long time, drinking tea. Despite Howard's bombshell, she was absorbed in a more personal drama. She, Lisa Campbell, had very nearly let Michael Delaney make love to her that night. Every moral principle, every emotional conviction she had upheld linking sex inextricably with love, had flown out of the window. Lust, that was what it had been. Not just on his part – that was to be expected – but, more disturbingly, on hers too. Pure, primitive, physical attraction, nothing more. And she couldn't even put all the blame on him. She had quite deliberately led him on, and if it hadn't been for Howard catching out Barbara and Steve Wainwright that night, she would by now, at this very moment, be lying vanquished in Michael's bed instead of sitting drinking tea in the kitchen.

A narrow escape or a missed opportunity? The former, she insisted to herself. How long would she have survived an affair with the likes of Michael Delaney? A few weeks? A couple of months? And what then? A restless quest for someone better, a quest that had driven Barbara to drink, nymphomania, and now drugs?

A violently passionate affair with Michael would, no doubt, be mind-blowing while it lasted. But, ultimately, the memory of it could blight her chances of achieving a realistic, long-term, loving relationship elsewhere. You couldn't have your cake and eat it, as Barbara had discovered. You settled for either excitement or security, but you couldn't have both.

In Lisa's passionate but practical nature, recklessness fought a constant pitched battle against innate common sense. In the last few months common sense, for a change, had been getting the upper hand. She had been maturing, or so she had thought. Until now, that is, Michael having just demonstrated that a minimum of effort on his part could propel her on a kamikaze course of emotional self-destruction. What, for her, had been an earth-shattering experience had, for him, been a routine seduction – and a disappointingly easy one at that. She had not exactly made it difficult for him. Her shame, however, was rational rather than instinctive. She had felt no shame lying in his arms, it had been natural, inevitable . . . Hot waves of memory washed over her. Canute-like, she ordered them back. Michael, assuredly, wasn't sitting up half the night reliving their encounter. He would be fast asleep by now, preparing himself for the rigours of the morrow. Poor Jamie, about to become a tug-of-love child. She didn't fancy his chances with either of his parents.

Yet again, she was consigned to Limbo. Days became weeks, and still she did not hear from Michael. Not surprising, perhaps, he had warned her he would be busy. Nevertheless, it annoyed her to feel that a man could be about to ravish her one minute, and apparently totally forget about her the next. Despite her efforts, she could not so easily forget him. She could still feel those strong arms around her, those confident, caressing hands, that warm, possessive mouth. She blushed as she imagined what might have been. She kept reminding herself how lucky she had been to be saved by the bell, reproaching herself for her wanton behaviour, regretting what a push-over he must have thought her. Reckless longings continued to grapple with common sense. Eventually common sense won the day — in a manner of speaking. Lisa visited her doctor.

One hot summer's afternoon near the end of term, Lisa was lingering outside the College building, deep in conversation with a fellow-student. Absorbed in talking shop, she did not at first register the loud hooting in the street, having learned by now to shut herself off from London traffic noise. Only when she heard a peremptory, and unmistakable, voice, yelling, 'Li — sa!' did she turn her head to see Michael's car sitting impatiently on a double yellow line, while a warden loomed on the horizon. Her class-mate promptly scurried off, looking suitably impressed.

'Get in!' barked Michael in a tone which brooked no argument. Clearly, he wasn't in a particularly good mood. His face was strained, haggard almost. Seeing this, Lisa wisely let her intended sarcasm die on her lips.

'Before you start having a sulk about not hearing from

132

me,' he pre-empted her, 'I ought to warn you that I've had a diabolical day and I'm not my usual carefree, charming self.' He gave her a menacing grin. 'What's in there this time?' he asked, indicating Lisa's ill-starred shopping trolley.

'Galantine of chicken. I've got to get it into a fridge quickly or the jelly will melt.'

'Well, you can get *it into* me quickly instead. I'm starving, I haven't eaten since last night.'

Plainly they were heading for Montpelier Gardens. What a nerve he had, fumed Lisa, always expecting her to be available. He hadn't even bothered to phone her first. If he had, she would have given some excuse. Well, probably.

Michael was, as he said, not as relaxed as usual, cursing violently at red traffic lights and indiscriminately abusing fellow-motorists. She was so used to seeing him totally nonchalant, casual and devil-may-care that this air of harassment quite unnerved her. She had a sudden, vivid inkling of how terrifying Michael would be in anger.

'Is Howard still staying with you?' she ventured, uncertain whether her curiosity would be rebuffed.

'No, he's moved into his club in town. I keep telling him he ought to clear off for a week or two. His nerves are shot to pieces. One of his married daughters lives in Guernsey. He might go and stay with her for a bit.'

His face softened. 'Sorry, Lisa, I'm being perfectly foul, I know. How have you been?'

The unexpected smile was so disarming that Lisa's chagrin melted and she smiled back.

'Thinking about you. I mean,' she added hurriedly, 'about how you were getting on, with Jamie and everything.'

Michael sighed. 'You'll be hearing all about that in a minute,' he said, his expression grim again. 'Get a move

133

on, you old ratbag!' he snarled at an unsuspecting pedestrian, mincing across the road with a waistcoated poodle in tow. Lisa giggled nervously. She was somewhat relieved when the drive was over.

There was nothing, of course, to eat with the galantine, and as a result they finished the lot between them, Michael devouring the lion's share. It was, Lisa admitted, a triumph, and Michael was quick to tell her so.

'You're a genius, Lisa,' he declared, leaning back contentedly in his chair. 'In fact, you're too good to be true. A wonderful cook, and beautiful, passionate, and virtuous with it.'

Lisa flushed. 'I suppose you're being sarcastic,' she snapped, flinching at his use of the word virtuous.

'Not in the least. If you're fretting about the other night, I take all the blame, or rather all the credit, for that. It may not have looked like it, but I was the one who seduced you. My tactics were brilliant, I thought. I made it look the other way round, didn't I?'

Lisa was speechless. The man really was totally cold-blooded.

'How *dare* you . . . ?' she spluttered.

'I'd dare a lot more than that, Lisa. Sooner or later, some blighter or other was bound to have his way with you. It was inevitable. I didn't see why it shouldn't be me, that's all.'

'You obviously think I was a pushover!'

'Far from it. If you were, someone would have got there long before I did. I must admit, though, I didn't realise just how innocent you actually are.'

'Was, you mean,' she bit back, furious.

'Are. Innocence plus passion is a very heady mixture, Lisa. You were irresistible. Do you regret it?'

'Regret what? What did happen, or what didn't?'

134

'I suspect you regret both. What a complicated little creature you are.'

Why did he have to look at her like that? Didn't he realise the effect it had? Of course he did, damn him! Lisa's scalp was tingling, her hands were trembling, and some trapped bird was flapping around inside her chest. She panicked. She mustn't let this conversation go any further. It was leading, inexorably, back into the bedroom. Reading her thoughts, he continued, 'Don't worry. I didn't bring you back here for that. Not right now, anyway.'

'I've got to go,' she blurted, standing up.

'Lisa, for God's sake, sit down, shut up, and listen.' His tone was suddenly cold, authoritative, impossible to disobey.

'Wainwright's moved in with Barbara, and it looks all set to stay that way. For how long is another matter, but they still seem to be in that first fine careless rapture. I've been making discreet enquiries about him through the media people I know. He turns out to be a nasty piece of work, debauched to the point of depravity. And if you think that's the pot calling the kettle black, let me tell you that I'm a regular boy scout compared to friend Wainwright. I won't shock you with all the sordid details. Let's just say he's not exactly a family man, and that every day Jamie spends under the same roof as him is a personal affront as far as I'm concerned.

'I went to see Barbara. I was very reasonable and calm about it all and suggested, quite casually, that Jamie spend a few weeks with my sister in Essex while the dust dies down. I thought she might buy it − having a kid around the place must cramp their style, and if it doesn't it bloody well ought to! God knows what sort of sex education Jamie's picking up with those two pawing each other all over the house. But she immediately went off the deep end — accused me of trying to get Jamie away from her and so on. She's never liked Sylvia much, of course, you'd hardly expect her to, but Jamie's often gone there in the school holidays and she's never objected before. No, she's afraid, quite rightly, that this time she might not get him back. Well, I played it cool and shrugged it off, to keep her off her guard. Then I went back to see my solicitor.'

He paused and lit a cigarette.

'I didn't think you smoked,' said Lisa, viewing it with distaste.

'I don't. I packed it in years ago, when I was in hospital. These are some Davina left lying about,' he explained brutally. 'Don't look so blooming sanctimonious, Lisa,' he snapped, his accent resurfacing under the strain. But, sighing, he extinguished it, and started pacing around the room instead.

'I told him about Barbara's drinking, drug-taking and morals. I told him that Howard was going to divorce her for adultery, and would oblige me by putting all the dirt in his affidavit. I told him I could afford to give my son the best of everything, that I'd financially supported him since he was born, that I'd visited him religiously practically every weekend, and that I'd pay the best legal brains in the country to get him back from Barbara. Do you know what he said?' His eyes were blazing.

'He said that as Jamie's only seven, had always lived with his mother, was well cared for, and because I'd been the guilty party in our divorce, it would take a very eccentric judge indeed to part him from her. Possession is, of course, nine points of the law. Besides which, he pointed out, Barbara could easily drum up counter-evidence and testimonials to discredit my attempts at character assassination. And for good measure, he felt that she'd have no difficulty in convincing a court, on the

136

evidence of our disastrous marriage, that I'm a footloose travelling man, a dyed-in-the-wool Casanova, hardly ever at home, and likely to prove an unfit father. To cap it all, she's got Daddy to pick up all the nasty old legal fees.'

'*You* were the guilty party?'

'Oh yes, in law. We agreed that it would be less damaging for Jamie as he grew up if I was officially the baddie. Boys come to terms pretty easily with their father's sins, given the double standard we all live by, and I didn't want him thinking ill of his mother. So she divorced me for adultery. There was, I admit, plenty of it once she'd walked out on me.'

'So it's hopeless then?'

'Of course it's not hopeless! I don't give up that easily. Lawyers are a cautious breed, like doctors. If I'd believed the doctors, I'd have died five years ago just to prove them right. No, I'm going to win this battle if it costs me every penny I have. But money's not enough. That's where you come in.' He impaled her with a look like a shaft of steel, that fixed her to her chair. She had a giddy sense of undefined premonition.

'Legally, it seems, I'd stand a much beter chance if I could present myself as a pillar of society, a solid family man, to squash Barbara's portrait of me as some swinging photographer type, jumping in and out of bed with all my models. No, what I need is a wife. And not just any wife. A wife beyond reproach, with an immaculate reputation, a respectable background, motherly, charming, sweet-natured, devoted to Jamie – and a good cook.'

Lisa was dumbstruck.

'In return,' he continued, not bothering to ratify the identity of the likely candidate, 'you can have anything you want – a house, domestic help, your own catering business . . .'

'Just wait a minute,' interrupted Lisa, her wits rapidly

137

restored, her voice frosty. 'What exactly are you suggesting?'

'I should have thought that was obvious. I'm asking you to marry me, dammit.'

'So that you can fool a judge, is that it? A marriage of convenience?'

'Certainly not. I mean marriage in every sense of the word. We might fool a judge, but we could never fool Jamie. There aren't any strings, Lisa. And this time, marriage means for life. I'm not putting Jamie through another divorce.'

'But we don't love each other!'

'There you go again. Love, love love! Look, Lisa, I actually *like* you. Jamie likes you. You turn me on, you don't know how much − yet. What more do you want? Gypsy violins?'

'Well, I'm absolutely bowled over, of course! What girl could resist such a proposal?'

'Lisa, give me some credit for honesty, at least. I could have given you a moonlight serenade, down on one knee with a rose between my teeth. Perhaps you might even have fallen for it, except that romantic protestations would sound plain ridiculous coming from someone like me. I'm neither a con-merchant nor the worst kind of fool − one who doesn't learn from experience. I loved Barbara, remember. You can see how far that got us. I won't be tempted to use sentimental code-words just to satisfy your youthful obsession with love!'

'I suppose you think insulting me will sway me in your favour! The answer is no. No, no, *no*!'

'Where do you think you're going?'

'Home. I suggest you visit a marriage bureau, or put your name into one of those computer dating machines.'

Michael was too quick for her. He got to the door first and stood barring her way, impassable as a drawbridge.

138

'Are you going to keep me here by force? Whether you say you love me or not is academic, in any case, because I most certainly don't love you!'

'I know that,' he soothed, with ominous quietness. 'But you like me too, don't bother to deny it. And you want me, almost as much as I want you.' His arms went round her, he pressed her head against his chest. 'Lisa,' he whispered, 'please help me. Please help Jamie.'

Her head started to swim. It was impossible to think clearly, locked against him, feeling the warmth of his body, with only their thin clothing separating flesh from flesh. The strength drained out of her. He started kissing her hair, his hands sending messages up and down her spine. Then he lifted her head and forced her to look into his eyes. Fatal, always fatal.

What was love, anyway? Or rather, what emotion was it that she saw in those jet-black orbs? Implacably, they seemed to be luring her into a dark, secret tunnel where unknown forces lurked, waiting to overpower her utterly. When he kissed her no more words were needed — it was an expression of desire, a plea for help, an explicit invitation, an assumption of surrender, all rolled into one. Lisa moaned.

'You wouldn't regret it, Lisa,' he murmured, kissing her throat as he unbuttoned her blouse.

'No, Michael,' she whimpered, aware that the protest was a formality. Maybe this was love after all, she thought desperately. Whatever it was, she had not learned anything from their last encounter because she had no armoury, no weaponry, against it. 'He wants to *marry* you,' an inner voice reminded her. That meant something, surely? What more binding commitment could he make? Other men might pretend love, to get you into bed, but never mention marriage. Desire blunted her

139

reason. What matter if they did not love each other? They both loved Jamie, didn't they?

Having lost the use of her legs, Lisa realised that they were lying, intertwined, on the thick white carpet. Every nerve in her body was screaming in anticipation. Very soon retreat would be impossible.

'Will you marry me, Lisa?' he murmured again, his voice like velvet. Everything was happening too fast, this time, it was already too late to resist him.

'Yes,' she groaned, her breath coming in gasps,her body helpless, her mind drugged. 'Yes', the magic word that would end this torment, bring her release. 'Yes', the ultimate surrender.

And then, abruptly, he picked her up off the floor, carried her to an armchair, and deposited her on it. Breathing rather heavily, he crossed to the window and stood with his back to her, looking out on the street. Lisa blinked, confused.

'W – why did you stop?' she squeaked, half-astonished, half-outraged.

'I've proved my point, I think.If you want me, Lisa, you're going to have to marry me before you can have me. I'm saving myself till after the wedding.'

'*What*?'

'Not concern for your virtue, sweetheart. I'm just giving you an incentive to co-operate. If I make love to you now, I'll want to again and again, and before I know it you'll have me on your terms, without a wedding ring. No, it's marriage or nothing, Lisa. What you might call sexual rôle reversal. So the sooner we get married, the better. You ought to phone your father and tell him right away. We don't want him thinking it's a shotgun job. I'll get Sylv and my old mum along, just so it's a proper wedding. I take it you don't want Jamie to be page boy?'

It was too much for Lisa. She burst into tears.

140

'I hate you!' she stormed, while allowing him to put his arms around her and wipe her eyes. 'I *hate* you!'

Michael smiled. 'Be careful, darling Lisa. That's very nearly the same thing as love.'

Chapter Eight

Michael gave her no time to think better of it. He immediately put through a long-distance phone call to Auchterbrae and formally asked Dr Campbell for his daughter's hand in marriage. Any half-hearted hopes Lisa might have had that he might play the heavy father and put a spoke in the arrangements were quickly dashed. Though understandably taken aback, he was impressed by Michael's courteous, mature tones, and, surprisingly, accepted the wedding's early date and Southern venue without demur, Michael's positive and forceful statement of their intentions making objections seem inappropriate. Indeed, he was quick to assure Michael that of course he would travel down for the ceremony, he had no doubt he could put up with Alistair Forsyth for a couple of nights. By the time Michael passed the telephone to Lisa, her blubbering incoherence merely served to provide further evidence that this thing was bigger than both of them.

That over, Michael called his mother, and then his sister, to announce his engagement. Their whoops of delight were audible across the room, and Lisa was again forced to take the receiver from him and accept the gleeful congratulations of two cheerful Cockney ladies who instantly behaved as if they had known her for years.

Mrs Delaney, incorrigibly, kept calling her 'Liza' and chuckled knowingly that she never thought anyone would ever get that no-good son of hers down the aisle again.

By the time Michael took her home there was, as he had intended, no going back.

'No need to look so sick,' he teased her, as he said goodnight. 'Although I suppose people will expect you to look pale and nauseous. Mum and Sylv will never believe you're not pregnant.'

Sarah, of course, was dumbstruck by the news. But if she nurtured the same suspicions as Mum and Sylv, she tactfully didn't voice them. No-one appeared to suspect Michael's true motive in marrying her – not even Howard, who, genuinely delighted, postponed his trip to Guernsey so that he could be best man. Sarah assumed, despite the Register Office nature of the ceremony, that she was to be some sort of honorary bridesmaid, and supervised the buying of a cream linen suit for Lisa, and the ordering of bouquets and buttonholes. While Lisa, punch drunk, looked on helplessly, the licence was obtained and arrangements finalised. On 28th July, the day before the Royal Wedding, she was destinined to become Mrs Michael Delaney. She would be in good company, Michael observed. All the best people were getting married that week.

He didn't let Lisa out of his sight more than was absolutely necessary, almost as if he were afraid she might run away. But, with every day that passed, Lisa found that she cared less and less why he was marrying her, and more and more that they would soon be man and wife. She was propelled by forces beyond her control, and could summon neither strength nor motivation to resist them. Her greatest, deepest anxiety was over what Jamie's reaction would be. They had put off telling him because Michael had, unaccountably, put off telling Barbara.

143

'I wish I could avoid her finding out until after the wedding,' he muttered. 'She's bound to be a perfect bitch about it and cause trouble if she possibly can − 'specially as she's likely to see it as a plot against her.'

'Well, isn't it?' pointed out Lisa boldly.

'Do you have to deprecate our marriage at every opportunity?' he asked her coldly. 'Are you planning to throw all that in my face every time we have a minor row?'

Chastened, Lisa fell silent.

'I'll tell her next Saturday,' continued Michael, 'when I go to fetch Jamie, or rather after I take him back. You can tell Jamie yourself. I want you here waiting for us.'

That Saturday morning Lisa let herself into Montpelier Gardens with her own latchkey and waited, quaking, to break the news to her future stepson. They were taking a picnic to Whipsnade, and she busily packed cold chicken and sausages, tomatoes, fruit, cans of drink and a flask of coffee. She encouraged herself, nervously, with the memory of how Jamie had cuddled up to her that night she had put him to bed. He was hardly what you'd call a demonstrative child, so this must surely have been a good sign. And then, of course, she did represent a reliable source of unlimited chips.

As the Bentleys' home in Holland Park was no distance by car, she was beginning to worry when Michael and Jamie had not appeared by eleven. When eventually Michael did arrive, she knew, heart-stoppingly, that all was not well. He was alone.

'Where's Jamie?' she blurted, immediately assuming the worst, that Barbara was denying access.

'Relax. He's in the car.' His voice was weary. 'Look, Lisa, Barbara already knew. My fault for putting it off. The damn grapevine as usual. Which means, of course, that Jamie already knew. He's playing up. Barbara's had her oar in with a vengeance. Don't take it personally. He

144

probably sees you as a rival for my affections or something. I guess we should have expected it. Just let it wash over you. He'll come round.'

Lisa felt the thud of a fear come true. 'You mean, he's anti?'

'Yes. I've threatened him with a good hiding if he gives you any lip. Don't over-humour him. He despises weakness.'

'What exactly did Barbara say?'

'Oh, she made a few cynical observations,' said Michael dismissively. 'But she's on some sort of high today. Looked as if she'd just popped something. Wainwright was still in bed, so I didn't have the pleasure of meeting him. She obviously couldn't wait to rejoin him there.'

Lisa went into the kitchen and began fiddling with the hamper to hide her distress.

'Michael,' she began hesitantly, 'if Jamie really doesn't like me, marrying me could achieve the opposite of what you intended. Barbara will take advantage of it in court. Sometimes the judge even questions the child.'

'Rubbish,' soothed Michael. 'You could be a bloke in drag before Jamie would prefer Babs and Wainwright to you and me.' He began kissing her neck from behind, caressing her breasts, murmuring, 'Only three more days, Lisa.'

Whenever she showed signs of wavering, he moved in with similar tactics, and to her repeated shame, they always succeeded. Well, at least Jamie wasn't being given right of veto. That must be some solace for her wounded pride.

Jamie parrotted a greeting to her after a warning glance from Michael, managing nonetheless to inject the salutation with covert hostility. Lisa sat in the back of the car with him and started enumerating the contents of the

145

hamper. Jamie displayed no interest but did not dare 'give her any lip'. Clearly he knew from experience that Michael did not make idle threats.

They stopped close to Whipsnade for petrol. Strangely, without his father for an audience, Jamie thawed enough to say, 'Steve's got knobbly knees.'

'What did you say?' asked Lisa, quite taken aback by this outlandish comment.

'When he's undressed, he's really skinny. He hasn't got muscles like my dad.'

Lisa coloured, glad that Michael was not in the car to hear his son's observations on Wainwright's unclothed physique.

'Barbara and him spend *hours* in the bathroom,' continued Jamie, unabashed. 'Brigitta says — '

The car door opened and Jamie reverted to dignified silence, leaving Lisa to ponder on just what indiscreet goings-on Jamie had been witnessing. She felt, also, that although Jamie was out to convince his father of his disapproval of his forthcoming marriage, his unprompted remarks to her had just indicated, obliquely, that he did not hold her to blame. Clearly Jamie had a suppressed need to talk to someone, to confide in an adult, and whatever confusion reigned in his childish thoughts, he was already too incipiently masculine to admit to any insecurities in front of his father. It would be a long hard struggle with Jamie, all right. His seven years had taught him to trust no-one but Michael. And now he had even let him down.

This momentary insight was mildly heartening, but, fearing to sound fanciful, Lisa was not inclined to share it with Michael. Amateur child psychology was, no doubt, a dangerous pastime.

The day was a strain, with Jamie testing both of them to the limits. He had a positive gift for going right up to the

146

line without quite overstepping it, leaving Michael exasperated but unable, in fairness, to retaliate. The classic example came when they got back to the flat and Jamie politely refused Lisa's offer of chips. It was the greatest snub he knew how to deliver. Michael took him home while Lisa cried her eyes out.

The next day, Michael and Lisa went to meet Dr Campbell at King's Cross. Despite his canny nature and customary Scots reserve, Lisa's father proved no match for the infinitely flexible Delaney charm. Lisa felt quite the outsider over dinner, as the two men chatted away on the usual male topics with the easy rapport of old comrades. She experienced some surprise at this, as superficially they had so little in common. As they dropped him off at Dr Forsyth's, he shook Michael's hand energetically and said in his forthright way, 'I'm glad to see two young people so obviously in love,' whispering in his daughter's ear for good measure, 'that's a fine figure of a man you've found for yourself, Lisa.'

'He likes you,' remarked Lisa dryly in the car going home. 'I thought he would put you down for a world-weary rake. How do you do it?'

'That's my girl, always piling on the compliments. I liked him too, actually. It'll be nice to have an old man again.'

'He thinks we look terribly in love,' pursued Lisa recklessly, knowing she was provoking him.

'Would you rather he didn't think it? Or that we didn't look it? Angling for another wee skirmish, are we?'

Lisa fell silent.

'I'll be up in town all day tomorrow,' continued Michael, 'tying up some loose ends so that we can have a week off. I'm afraid that's all I can spare — I didn't get much chance to plan in advance, did I?'

'You mean, we're having a honeymoon?'

'Don't you want one? Just a friend's villa in the South of France, I hope that'll do. Very isolated, with its own pool. No need to pack any clothes. Just bring your handbag and a toothbrush.'

He gave her a brief, hard kiss and let her out of the car.

'I'll be round at about six tomorrow,' he said. 'We'll go out to eat. I don't trust myself alone in the flat with you.'

Lisa found a note from Sarah on the kitchen table saying that she wouldn't be back that night. She had all but moved in with Richard of late, so there was nothing unusual about her absence. Irrationally, Lisa balked at the prospect of being alone in the flat all night, but then, after tomorrow, she wouldn't be alone at night any more. The familiar blend of anticipation and doubt churned round inside her.

Increasingly, she had succumbed to a sense of unreality, as if she were the passive observer of unstoppable events affecting a third party. Pre-wedding nerves, she reasoned. 'No such thing,' her heart told her. 'You're biting off more than you can chew and you know it – taking on a ruthless, determined man and a disturbed, damaged child, providing a sex object for one and an unwanted stepmother for the other.'

'It's not too late,' a small voice reminded her. 'You can still pull out. Confide in your father.'

She passed her hand across her brow. She felt weak, dazed, confused. This marriage was for life, he had said. Not as a token of undying love, fidelity, or faith in the future, just as a bald statement of intent: 'I'm not putting Jamie through another divorce.'

But what if he failed to get custody? Would the marriage be for life then? If only Michael were less brutally honest, less painfully uncompromising, she would at least be able to absolve herself of responsibility – the poor, deceived, besotted virgin versus the vile seducer. But it wasn't like that at all. It was the spider saying to the fly, 'Come into my parlour so I can eat you up.' And the fly obliging without so much as a struggle.

She was unpinning her hair and preparing to get undressed when the doorbell rang. Puzzled, she put down her brush and went to answer it. Perhaps Sarah had had a tiff with Richard and had forgotten her key. Unsuspecting in her preoccupied state, she opened the door wide without thinking, allowing Barbara to walk straight in.

Her face was white, pinched, vicious.

'Is Michael here?' she asked immediately.

'N – no,' admitted Lisa, gulping.

Barbara sat down unbidden and lit a cigarette. It had a sweet, sickly smell which Lisa did not recognise. She inhaled deeply.

'Got anything to drink?' she asked insolently. Lisa found it hard to adjust to her erstwhile employer in the rôle of uninvited guest.

'I think there's some sherry,' she mumbled, wishing desperately that Michael *was* here, or that he would phone, as he usually did after he got home, to wish her a sexy goodnight.

'That'll do,' purred Barbara, flashing her a sudden, vapid smile. Lisa fetched it and sat down opposite her, ready for an outburst, an attack, threats, insults, intimidation.

'Mrs Bentley,' she begun, 'I really don't wish us to be enemies . . .'

'Why is he marrying you?' demanded Barbara, going straight to the point. 'I can't believe you're pregnant, Michael's not that green. And please don't take it personally, but I can't believe he's in love with you either.'

'Why shouldn't he be? I happen to love him!' Lisa bit her lip. What on earth had made her say that? It hadn't been necessary.

Barbara laughed rather unpleasantly. 'Charming, Lisa, dear, I know just how you're feeling, believe me. I've been there too, remember. Pretty hot stuff, isn't he? Not that you've had anyone to compare him with, of course.'

Lisa blushed furiously. Barbara put down her cigarette and moved next to her, taking hold of her arm with a bird-like grip. Lisa saw that Barbara was shaking.

'I'll tell you why he's marrying you, in case you haven't realised. Because he wants a nanny for James. Because he hates me, and he hates Steve, and he and Howard between them will do everything they possibly can to take my child away from me.' Lisa tried to move away. 'Please hear me out,' pleaded Barbara, her voice constricted.

'I know Howard won't come back, I should never have married him anyway. And Steve won't stay with me for long, I know that too. I'd have a better chance with Steve if I let James go – he loathes children. But James really matters to me, Lisa – more than Michael, Howard, Steve, or all the others put together. He's mine, and I love him. You've never had a child, you can't begin to understand how it feels, to have people trying to turn him against me.

'Whatever Michael would like to believe, James doesn't want to leave me either. Ever since he got wind of what's going on he's been having nightmares, wetting the bed, refusing food. He's afraid, Lisa. How would you like it if they'd threatened to take you away from your mother when you were seven years old? However tough he tries to look, he's just a little boy, and he *needs* me. Michael thinks I'm a useless mother, I know, and okay, you'd probably be better at it than me. But not with my child! Give him another child, Lisa, but please, please, let me keep mine!'

Barbara burst into a violent fit of sobbing, real, stormy

tears staining her silk blouse and smudging her make-up. She looked suddenly ten years older, frightened, vulnerable.

'Promise me, Lisa,' pleaded Barbara. 'Marry him if you must, but talk him out of this wicked, cruel plan of his! Don't let him say dreadful things about me in court. James would be bound to hear about it, sooner or later. How would you have liked your mother's name dragged through the mud?'

Despite the lack of any point in comparison between Barbara and Lisa's mother, a gentle, unassuming and industrious soul who would have been appalled at this ghastly mess, Lisa felt shocked and shaken to see the situation so vividly from Barbara's point of view. True enough, Jamie hadn't welcomed his father's remarriage. He was not the type of child to display disturbed behaviour unless there were some deep-rooted and drastic cause for his distress. And while Barbara might, when it suited her, be an accomplished play-actress, there was no doubting the authenticity of her anguish.

'Promise me,' she gasped again, her grip painfully tight. Lisa felt helpless, hopeless.

'I can't promise,' she stated, woodenly. 'I have no influence over Michael. He does exactly as he likes, you of all people should know that. And having another baby wouldn't make the slightest difference. He wants Jamie and he means to have him.' She paused, alarmed at how brutal the truth sounded.

'You bitch,' seethed Barbara, changing mood abruptly, standing up and wiping her eyes angrily with the back of her hand. 'Don't try that line with me. "I'm awfully sorry, Mrs Bentley, but there's nothing I can do." Don't try to duck out of your part in all this. His only chance of custody is a neat little wife like you. The usual tarts he picks up wouldn't do at all – oh, no! He's got

151

you well duped, hasn't he? I just hope he gives you the hell he gave me!'

The phone started to ring. Numbly, Lisa went to answer it.

'Yes, I'm in bed. Yes, everything's fine. Goodnight.'

Barbara smirked. 'Checking up on you already, is he? Think about what I said, Lisa. Remember, whatever happens will be on your conscience too.' Leaving her cigarette still smouldering and her sherry untouched, Barbara flung Lisa a look of pure hatred.

'God help you,' she said bitterly, 'when *you* have a baby and when *you* decide you can't take it any more. Has it occurred to you that one day you could be in my shoes, fighting to keep the child you gave birth to? And make no mistake, I'm going to fight. I'll die before I let Jamie go!'

The door slammed. Lisa sat shattered, Barbara's words echoing in the empty room. The last few weeks did a jumbled action replay inside her head, fragments of conversations, frozen images, remembered sensations crowding in on her tormented mind like bees buzzing in a hive. She began trembling uncontrollably. In thirty-six hours, she would be married.

She realised with a sudden sense of icy calm, that she could not go through with it. Like a sleepwalker, she stumbled towards the phone and began dialling Michael's number, recalling, absurdly, the first time she had ever done so. As if in mockery of her reminiscence, she got the Ansaphone. Thwarted, she put the receiver back. He had been at home only a few moments ago. Where had he gone at this time of night? So absorbed was she in her thoughts, so deep in her dilemma, that she did not immediately register the doorbell ringing until it was followed up by loud knocking and Michael calling 'Lisa!' through the letter-box. Her limbs froze at the prospect of what she must say to him. She let him in.

'What in hell's been going on?' he asked immediately, taking in her stricken expression. He sniffed the air. 'You shouldn't let Sarah smoke that stuff in the flat, Lisa,' he commented, walking into the living-room. He looked for a moment at the glass of sherry and the still-smouldering cigarette, and then, with a muttered oath of exasperation, turned to Lisa accusingly.

'Barbara,' he said. 'She was here when I rang, wasn't she? You sounded sort of strangled on the phone, I knew something was wrong. I imagined some burglar had you at knifepoint. That's why I came back.'

'I'm not going to marry you, Michael,' announced Lisa bleakly, her incorrigible habit of frank speaking sounding hideously discordant. She should have put it more subtly, she thought, built up to it slowly, tactfully, explained her reasons. One didn't go about jilting a man in such heavy-handed fashion. How exactly did one go about jilting a man? she wondered. She started laughing, the strange, off-key laugh of burgeoning hysteria.

'I was waiting for this,' said Michael quietly. 'What line did she give you? The maternal agony bit, right? "Take everything I have, but not my adored child. Do not be a party to this evil plot to part mother and son.'' Right? *Right*!' He seized her by the shoulders. The pain brought her to her senses.

'It's not because of Barbara,' she said, her voice sounding alien to her, the words coming from some source outside her head. 'It's because of *me*. I've been a coward and a fool. And you're nothing but a very clever bully.' She drew herself up to her full height. 'Jamie isn't my responsibility. I won't take on board his problems, your problems, Barbara's problems. I'm not ending up a nervous wreck like her. I won't be used! I have my pride!' Buried reserves of Celtic defiance came to her aid, green eyes flashing wildly out of the pallor of her face. Michael might be strong, but she would prove she was no weakling, however successfully he had contrived till now to bend her will to this.

'Don't be ridiculous,' he snapped, releasing her. 'You're over-dramatising everything. Barbara's neurosis is catching, it seems. She must have given you a real basinful in the short time she was here. I feel like going round there and belting her.'

'Michael, in a few moments I am going to pick up that telephone and call my father. I'm going to ask him to take me back home with him tomorrow.'

Something unfamiliar in the steely quality of her voice must have finally convinced him. His eyes turned to granite.

'You really mean it, don't you?' he asked, wonderingly. She nodded, experiencing an odd thrill at the hollowness of his voice, the pain behind his eyes. If only he loved me, she thought, with startling clarity, I could never let him go!

He turned his back on her, his head bowed in thought. There was a long, electric silence. When he turned round to speak, his face was terrifying.

'You're overlooking one small point, Lisa. I'm not a gentleman, remember? I have no scruples. I always get what I want and I fight dirty if that's the price of winning. You were a fool to trust me, sweetheart.'

'I don't trust you!' she countered automatically frightened as she saw before her the other Michael, the one who had always been just visible below the surface charm – ruthless, insensitive, and hard as nails. 'I never trusted you!'

'Oh, but you did. I have in my possession, Lisa, some exquisite and supremely tasteful pictures of you. You trusted me enough to sign a blanket release form. I, in turn, can sign those pictures over to an agency, and they

154

can do with them what they will. The whole question of good taste depends on context, and presentation. Certain publications have a knack for improving on the original negatives. The camera may not lie, but it's wonderful what you can do in a darkroom.'

Lisa didn't move. 'You're trying to blackmail me?' she asked, her voice heavy with scorn.

'Quick on the uptake, aren't you? Right first time.'

'You wouldn't do it. Unscrupulous you may be, but you'd never see your own work degraded.'

'No-one would recognise the finished product as my work, I can assure you. Certain people would, however, recognise you. Quite an eye-opener for your dear old dad and the folks back home.'

'My father, and people in Auchterbrae, would never look at − that kind of thing.'

'Wouldn't they just? Dreadful nuisance, isn't it, unsolicited mail?'

Lisa's lip curled with contempt. 'It won't work, Michael. Not even you would sink that low. If necessary, I shall call your bluff.'

'You don't know me at all well, do you, Lisa? You really think I'm going to stand by and let you throw me over, make a fool of me in front of my family, my friends, my son, my ex-wife, just because Barbara's been playing games with your oh-so-delicate conscience? You think I'd let that go unpunished? Don't test me, Lisa. I never say things I don't mean. I'm not a nice person. In fact, I'm an absolute bastard. You should never have dared me to prove it.'

If he'd shouted or raged, she would have feared him less. But something horribly controlled, frighteningly malevolent, in his voice and eyes left her hypnotised, like a rabbit confronting a snake. As he closed in relentlessly

155

on his prey, she stood rooted to the spot. He trapped her in strong, merciless arms.

'My tactics were well off the mark, it seems,' he observed. 'I've been behaving too well for my own good. Perhaps I should start showing myself in my true colours.' He began methodically pulling her clothes off her, quite roughly, wrenching her arms away as she tried to resist him.

'Stop it,' she gasped, strangling a cry of fear.

'Poor Lisa,' he mocked. 'I really had you fooled, didn't I? Thought I was basically a decent chap, did you? You were wrong.'

He scooped her up like a sack of feathers and kicked open the door of her bedroom, dropping her ungently on to the bed while he removed his own clothing, never taking his eyes off her.

'You — you're not going to r-rape me?' hissed Lisa, recognising the utter powerlessness of her position, her eyes transfixed on him as he stripped.

'It all depends on what you mean by rape,' he replied, his tone quite crisp and matter-of-fact. 'If you insist on struggling, I suppose that's what it'll be.'

'You wouldn't!'

'So you keep saying. "You wouldn't! You wouldn't!" You've got such a touching high opinion of me, I never realised what girlish illusions you were cherishing. Time you grew up, Lisa.'

With a blood-curdling sense of revelation, Lisa knew that Michael was not bluffing. This was for real.

And this was for real as well, his body stretched out against hers, the hair on his chest rough against her breasts, his hands doing what they pleased. She lay rigid. Let him go ahead and rape her. She would not respond. The fluttering in her stomach was fear, nothing more.

'Just lie back and think of Scotland,' he mocked.

'You're not supposed to enjoy it the first time, so don't let that worry you.'

For a man bent on violence, he had a very light touch. His lips and hands explored her idly, teasingly, with all the proprietorial candour of a husband. He made no allowances whatsoever for her innocence. The things he did shocked, appalled and delighted her, all in one. She remained motionless, hands clenched. But there were other parts of her hopelessly beyond any voluntary control.

'If I didn't know that you were hating every minute of this,' he taunted her, 'I could swear you were getting just a little bit excited.'

'I'll never forgive you, never,' seethed Lisa. But he just laughed softly and continued to torment her, as if determined to put off the evil moment, out of spite.

Inexorably, Lisa was losing control. Strange chemicals were seeping into her bloodstream, triggering off reactions, detonating fuses, all over her body. She moaned helplessly.

'Poor baby,' remarked Michael, with exaggerated sympathy. 'I'm suddenly stricken by conscience pangs.' He drew back. 'Perhaps I should redeem myself by leaving you intact. That is what you want, isn't it? *Isn't it*?'

Despair overcame her as she realised she was beaten. He had done this to her once before, but not like this. Not when she was at fever pitch, every recess of her treacherous body throbbing with expectation.

Convulsively, she threw her arms around him, and then no more words were spoken. She hurtled into a vortex of sensation, heard her own voice crying out, and then was blind and deaf to everything except the passion that engulfed her.

He didn't stay the night. He got dressed, and kindly,

but coolly, pulled the covers over her and wished her sweet dreams. Lisa was spent, ashamed of her weakness, angry that he had exploited it, tingling with the afterglow of slaked desire.

He looked hard into her eyes before he left. They were still unfathomable, black, sinister pools of ink.

'Run out on me now, Lisa,' he said softly, 'and I'll make you sorry. Sleep tight.' And he was gone.

Stepping out of the Register Office into the sunshine, Lisa smiled for the camera. Richard was leaping about in extrovert fashion, taking the wedding photographs: Lisa, slightly dazed, red hair vivid against the cream linen, Michael, sanguine and determined in a dark suit and tie, Howard looking avuncular and bemused, Sylvia and her husband, Len, beaming widely, Dr Campbell gazing wistfully, Sarah with a bright, envious grin, and Mrs Delaney senior sniffing luxuriously into her hanky.

They had an early lunch at a hotel, Lisa twisting her platinum wedding band nervously under the tablecloth. She had not seen Michael since the shattering events of Sunday night – he had cancelled their date for the previous evening, curtly explaining that he had work to finish. She was vaguely aware of her father and Howard making speeches, and Michael delivering a witty reply. Michael's mother, sitting next to Lisa, was a garrulous old bird, and hissed advice conspiratorially at her new daughter-in-law throughout the meal.

'You just stand up to him, Liza love,' she counselled, 'and you'll do all right. That Babs just let him walk all over her. Give 'im 'ell, gel! He can take it.' And she gave Lisa's hand an encouraging squeeze.

The advice from Sylvia was strangely different. Catching Lisa in the powder-room, she gave her an affectionate hug and looked at her appraisingly with the

158

familiar black Delaney eyes. Fortyish, motherly, and a bit on the plump side, Sylvia would be a dangerously easy person to confide in.

'You look a bit peaky, pet,' she probed, tactfully omitting any suggested diagnosis for this condition.

'Just wedding nerves,' smiled Lisa evasively. 'I don't kid myself marriage to Michael is going to be a bed of roses.'

Sylvia chuckled. 'Mick always was a bit of a swine,' she remarked cheerfully, 'no use denying it. But underneath all the swagger, Lisa, he's been badly hurt. I never thought he'd ever trust a woman enough to get married again. He must have fallen for you good and proper. Be kind to him, won't you, love? He doesn't expect it, that's why he's not always kind himself. Try not to hurt him back. He'll be testing you all the time at first, it's his way.'

Lisa gulped miserably. Everyone was so busy assuming that Michael loved her. No-one, apart from Barbara, guessed at the truth, the sham behind the wedding. Even Michael believed, mistakenly, that he had blackmailed her into marriage. What he didn't know, and what she would never tell him, was that she had married him for one reason and one reason only. One that had revealed itself to her belatedly, out of a painful process of self-examination.

Yes, he had proved to her that he was utterly ruthless. Yes, he had convinced her that his threats had been genuine. Yes, his will was immeasurably stronger than her own. But, in a moment of devastating insight, Lisa had come to understand that weak, intimidated, and helpless though she might appear, she was still a Campbell. And no-one, not even Michael, forced a Campbell into a loveless marriage. Love ... the unmentionable word. Love ... one-sided, agonising, tyrannical. She had married, in despair, out of love.

159

They flew to Nice first class. Michael, visibly more relaxed now and in typically provocative mood, amused himself by flashing lascivious smiles at the stewardesses, who practically fell over themselves in their eagerness to answer his call button. He made Lisa take advantage of the free champagne, cheerfully describing the villa to her without bothering to hide that he had vacationed there before. Lisa did not ask with whom. She quaked slightly at the thought of a week's enforced idleness alone with Michael. She was bound to give herself away. To win his love had become the latest, most extravagant, of her day-dreams, one which she would certainly have no chance of realising unless she successfully hid her own feelings from that knowing, satirical gaze.

Resolving to behave like a mature woman and not an infatuated young bride, she acknowledged, despondently, that it was just not in her nature to pretend. And Michael was not an easy person to deceive.

The villa was about twenty miles from Nice airport − a white, sprawling, one-storey house of ultra-modern design, luxuriously appointed and stunningly located in a secluded, elevated position affording breathtaking views of the Mediterranean. It belonged, Michael explained, to a French newspaper proprietor who had once commissioned a photo-feature on the Foreign Legion.

'You do get around, don't you?' observed Lisa dryly, trying to hide her nerves as she took in the circular bed, mirrored ceiling, and an en suite sunken bath complete with jacuzzi. Michael grinned.

'The maid's been told to come in between eight and nine while we're out at dinner,' he informed her wickedly, 'so we'll be totally undisturbed. As for the telephone, no-one at home knows where we are.'

Lisa continued to unpack methodically.

'You won't be needing all that lot,' he mocked. 'I don't

think we'll have time for many sightseeing trips.'

'Sarah packed for me,' said Lisa brusquely, ignoring him. Michael picked up a white bikini between finger and thumb.

'What's this for?' he continued. 'There's only you and me invited to the party, sweetheart.'

'Give it back, Michael,' she snapped crossly, snatching it from him. He shrugged good-naturedly.

'Wear it if you like. I'll just have to take it off once we're in the water, won't I?' He smiled dangerously and began undressing. 'Personally, I can't wait to have a swim, cavorting around all day in this damn suit and tie. Lovely wedding, didn't you think? I thought we made a charming couple. Too bad St Paul's was already booked, but you can't have everything.' Instinctively, Lisa looked away, blushing, as he unzipped his trousers. She heard him laugh.

'See you in the pool,' he stated, opening the French doors and walking out, unabashedly naked. Sitting weakly on the bed, Lisa watched him covertly as he strode towards the water, silhouetted against the setting sunlight. He was, without doubt, a magnificent specimen, the ugly scars on his back somehow enhancing the uncompromising maleness of his body. He plunged into the glittering water and began swimming strongly with long, powerful strokes. Lisa looked at her bikini. It was, she supposed, rather ridiculous in the circumstances to insist on putting it on. But she couldn't bring herself to walk the fifty-odd feet towards the pool with nothing on. She hung up her linen suit with care, undressed, and then, making herself a sarong out of a giant, fluffy bath towel, took a deep breath and went to join him.

Paradoxically, Lisa felt her guilty secret was safe only when they were making love. Then, she could be excused a show of uninhibited feeling, which could be explained away as part of the intense physical interaction between them. The rest of the time, there was always a curious tension in the air, a holding back, a loss of the easy banter they had enjoyed earlier in their relationship.

They slept, ate, swam, sunbathed, and made love. But mostly, they made love. It encroached on all the other activities, even the eating. They showed a marked propensity for leaving restaurants hurriedly before considering the desserts, having a better one in view than any on the menu. Physical intimacy blotted out the fear and doubt. Lisa sought it like a drug to deaden pain. She noticed, increasingly, Michael's tendency to be abstracted, preoccupied, irritable even. She took the easy way out, getting round him the one certain way she knew how. But the deeper closeness of mind and heart and spirit eluded her. In many ways, she discovered, she and Michael were strangers. Their bodies had no secrets from each other, but their souls were miles apart. He seemed to prefer things that way, neatly rebuffing her attempts to reach inside his thoughts.

Nuzzling up to him drowsily one night, she ventured, 'How do I compare with Barbara?'

'Bloody hell, Lisa, what a question!'

'I need to know,' she persisted, half-shyly, her fingers tracing a teasing path down his chest and stomach.

'You mean in bed, I suppose?'

'Well, I know I'm a better cook, and I know she's better looking. Of course I mean in bed!'

'I haven't slept with Barbara for over five years. Tell you what, I'll do a bit of revision when we get back to London, and then give you my verdict.'

'Do be serious, Michael. It's only natural I should ask. You told me once she was sensational.'

'Fishing for compliments already? What a conceited

little thing you are. She's had more men than you've cooked hot dinners. Practice makes perfect, you know.'

Lisa took her hand away and turned her back on him.

'Sulk if you like. You asked for it.'

'Why do you always have to be so brutally honest?'

'Why do you always have to ask such awkward questions? Barbara is ancient history. Would you like me to compare you to all the others as well, and mark you all out of ten?'

Lisa hunched herself up rebelliously on her side of the bed. Michael took hold of her from behind and dragged her back beside him.

'Listen, Lisa. It's quite a challenge, going for a swim with a man-eating shark. But it's much more fun with a dolphin.'

'Safer, you mean.'

'Sure, it's safer. But at the end of the day, who wants it bitten off?'

'Must you be so crude?'

'Must you be so stupid?'

And, again, reassurance came with action, not words.

Chapter Nine

The day of their return to London arrived dispiritingly
quickly. The reality of the future was dampening. How
would this bizarre partnership adapt to everyday life, to
work, other people, Jamie, the bitter custody battle
ahead? You couldn't spend your entire married life in
bed, thought Lisa. The real tests were still to come.

Emptying the drawer of the dressing-table into her
suitcase, her thoughts far away, she stopped short on
noticing the foil packet of tiny pills. Typical, she thought,
cursing herself heartily. Still trying to adjust to an
unfamiliar habit she had, with the absent-mindedness
which had so often been her undoing, forgotten all about
them for the last two, no three, days. Popping a double
dose into her mouth hurriedly, she dismissed this
characteristic lapse with a philosophical shrug. After all,
she was a married woman now.

Michael seemed ill at ease on the journey home, his
excessive and unaccustomed politeness to her putting her
on edge. She much preferred him casual, tactless, rude
even. Naturally he was preoccupied, she thought, facing
as he did more meetings with his lawyers, his usual
crammed work schedule, and the prospect of the radical
change in life style which would accompany the voluntary
sacrifice of his freedom. Lisa, on the other hand, faced

several more weeks of leisure before the last term of her course began in the autumn.

She wasn't sure what she would do with so much spare time. Her solitary catering expeditions hardly seemed appropriate for the wife of a well-known and successful photojournalist. Michael had already indicated, rather scathingly, that he wasn't having her doing other people's washing up, and told her brusquely to come up with some ideas for putting other girls out to work for her. Sensibly, Lisa realised that she would do well to obtain her diploma before getting carried away by inflated ambitions. She didn't want Michael investing in a project which was other than reasonably watertight.

No, she would use the time prudently — in getting to know Jamie better, for example, in winning him over. Undoubtedly the way to her husband's heart was through his son. She would invite the help of Michael's mother and sister, they probably understood him better than anyone. She would also do her best to heal the rift with Barbara. By hook or by crook, she would make her marriage a success. So many resolutions . . .

They took a taxi from Heathrow back to Kensington. It was a stifling hot, sticky day. London had been beset by a heatwave. The air hung thick and heavy over the capital, its streets still festooned with tattered bunting.

After paying the driver, Michael bundled Lisa into the tiny lift with the suitcases, and shot off up the stairs to meet her at the top. Opening the door of the flat, they stepped over a huge heap of mail. Remembering himself, he ushered her out again and unceremoniously carried her back over the threshold.

'Welcome home, Mrs D.,' he remarked satirically, adding, 'make some coffee, there's a love,' as he began sifting through the post, dropping half of it, unopened, into the wastepaper basket. He sat down to read the rest, rewinding the tape on the answering machine as he did so.

When Lisa emerged from the kitchen with the coffee, Michael was standing with his back to her making a phone call. There was something strangely rigid about his shoulders, the tilt of his head. Normally he used the telephone while sprawled out full-length on the settee.

'I just heard the message,' he was saying, his voice hard but totally steady. 'Where is he? Good, I'll drive over there later. Yes . . . no . . . are you okay? Yes, I'd better. I'll be right over. 'Bye.'

When he turned to Lisa, his face was drained of colour, his eyes hollow.

'That was Howard,' he said tonelessly. 'Poor bloke never got to Guernsey, after all.' He sat down, dazed. Lisa didn't speak. She knew in a flash that something dreadful had happened, but she couldn't find her voice.

'Barbara's dead.' Lisa gasped. 'So's Wainwright. Car smash, a couple of days after we left. There's going to be an inquest. Wainwright was driving, drinking as well, it seems. They took the couple in the other car with them. All killed instantly.'

'Jamie . . . ?'

'He was safely at home with Brigitta, thank God.' Michael shuddered. 'Howard's sent him to Sylvia's.'

He gave Lisa a very odd look, his eyes shuttered, his voice sharp.

'Don't say it. Pity it didn't happen a bit sooner, eh? Seems I made you marry me for nothing. Let that be a lesson to both of us.'

Lisa stood, stunned.

'I've got to go over and see Howard. I'll phone Sylvia from his place. Better if you don't come. Everyone will be pretty het up, and none of it's really your problem.'

The words cut through her like jagged glass.

166

'If I'm going to be late, I'll ring you,' he said, giving her a brief kiss.

'I'm coming with you,' she blurted, unwilling to let him go alone, the vacant quality of his expression filling her with alarm.

'No,' he said flatly. 'Stay at home and warm my slippers, there's a good wife.'

The door slammed shut.

Delayed action shock took hold of her. Barbara – the same beautiful, dazzling, tormented Barbara who had accosted her, pleaded with her, berated her ten days before – was now pointlessly, violently, tragically dead. Wainwright, drunk at the wheel, had killed her, along with two other innocent people. Jamie could have been in the car with them. An icy shiver ran down her back. She found herself crying jerkily, the two cups of coffee cooling untouched, the suitcases with their Air France labels standing forlorn in the middle of the room, her wedding ring glinting in the dusty sunlight. How must Michael be feeling, faced suddenly with the death of the woman he had loved? Shattered, guilty, relieved? Resentful, perhaps, that Barbara, by her premature demise, had had the last laugh on his strategic remarriage? 'I'll die,' she had said, 'before I let Jamie go.' And true to her word, she had.

The next days were a nightmare. The full burden of the tragedy seemed to fall on Michael, as the one most able to shoulder it. It fell to him to support a devastated Howard, attend the inquest, despatch Brigitta back to Munich, and cope with Jamie, who had reacted to his mother's death far worse than anyone could have expected.

Tired and strained, Michael explained to a white-faced Lisa that he felt it best for everyone if Jamie remained with Sylvia for a while.

'It's neutral territory,' he explained. 'Coming here, at

167

this stage, would be like betraying his mother, you can see that, can't you? He's not emotionally mature enough to handle it. He's confused enough as it is.'

Lisa nodded bleakly.

'He's insisting on coming to the funeral,' continued Michael. 'It's probably best to let him. Lisa, I think it would be better if you weren't there.'

'Why? I was never Barbara's enemy. I ought to come. What will it look like if I don't? I am your wife, after all.'

'Don't act slighted. I'm thinking of Jamie.'

Something snapped. Lisa, for days now the model of wifely solicitude, of forbearance, of understanding, of tact – all of which had been a struggle – suddenly flared up.

'*I'm* thinking of Jamie! *I'm* going to be his mother now, remember? Why should I hide from a child? What will he think of me if I seem afraid to face him?'

Michael, unprepared for her outburst, gave in. 'As you wish,' he said tersely. 'You'd better go out and get yourself a black dress, then, hadn't you?'

Lisa supposed it was only natural that Michael should be temporarily uninterested in her sexually. He came to bed late and slept fitfully. He seemed to be in some state of inner torment, understandable, she reasoned, in the circumstances. Just a kind word, an affectionate caress, would have satisfied her, but he became increasingly withdrawn, his attitude towards her wavering between tolerant indifference and suppressed hostility. Lisa bore it all patiently, hoping that the long-delayed funeral would expunge the horror, and that afterwards everyone would start to readjust and take up the threads of normal life again.

But she was over-optimistic. Michael's instincts had been right, her presence at the funeral was a mistake. Jamie, holding his father's hand tightly and manfully

168

keeping back his tears, watched his mother's coffin lowered into the earth, only the trembling of his lower lip betraying the grief within. He refused stalwartly even to look at Lisa. Every tragedy needed its scapegoat. No matter that Steve Wainwright, with three times the legal limit of alcohol in his blood, was emphatically, and justly, the villain of the piece. Wainwright, for his sins, was dead. And Lisa, rightly or wrongly, was next in line.

Numb with the feeling of rejection, Lisa stood woodenly, outwardly composed, at Michael's side. As the minister intoned, blinding truth dawned over a grey horizon. Her marriage was doomed. Jamie would never accept her now, and Michael had realised, too late of course, that he need never have married her. It was one of life's classic little ironies that she, who was to have helped him regain his son, now effectively stood between them.

Sylvia, watching Lisa, seemed to read her thoughts.

'Speak no ill of the dead,' she remarked consolingly to Lisa, as they walked back to the waiting cars, 'but it might just be for the best. Don't worry about Jamie, pet. All the Delaney men are stubborn, but they're softies underneath. He owes it to his mother, to take it out on you, but he'll come round in his own good time. Just be patient. Remember, Michael loves you.'

Jamie, desperately struggling not to cry, gratefully let himself be driven away by his aunt and uncle, before whom he could weep without shame. Following his example, Lisa strove to keep her emotions in check. Michael would have had enough by now of people breaking down all around him. Tomorrow, she told herself, clinging to Sylvia's words for comfort, they would start their marriage afresh.

When she woke the next morning, Michael, as usual, was already up. She could hear him moving about in the bathroom. She lay silently wondering whether it would be good policy to take the initiative and inveigle him back into bed. She decided against it. If he wasn't in the mood, it would be crass to try to act the great temptress. A few more days, she told herself, and things would come right.

She feigned sleep as he walked back in, watching him dress from underneath her lids. A wave of hopeless longing swept through her. She shut her eyes tight. Suddenly, she could sense him standing over her, looking down at her apparently sleeping face. Ashamed of her duplicity, she opened her eyes.

'Good morning,' she smiled shyly.

'Good morning, Mrs D.' He sat down on the bed and took her hand. Her heart jumped.

'Lisa, we have to have a serious talk,' he began, holding her hand in both of his. She felt her whole body go cold.

'W-what about?'

He looked at her penetratingly.

'When I bulldozed you into marrying me,' he said carefully, 'I wasn't thinking straight. I can see that now. I've never had much of a conscience, I admit that, but my sins have never found me out in quite this way before.'

'What sins?'

'Selfishness for one, dishonesty for another. You surely don't need me to make a full confession. You of all people should know what I'm talking about. I forced you into this, Lisa, and because I never lied to you about my motives, I fancied that made it a fair deal. You were right to try to pull out. It was despicable of me to blackmail you as I did. I would never have prostituted those pictures, Lisa, but of course you weren't to know that.'

I didn't marry you because of that, she wanted to say. I married you in spite of it, I couldn't help myself. But she said nothing.

'If I were religious, I'd see this whole damned mess as

170

God's punishment. Even though I'm not, I want to try to put things right if I can. Lisa, if you want to go, I'll set you free. If not, of course, I'll honour my obligations to you.'

Lisa swallowed hard.

'Set me free? You mean, split up? Already?'

'Don't make it sound so dramatic. As things are, I haven't yet had time totally to louse up your life. If you get out now, you've got a chance of putting the whole sordid business behind you. I've abused you, Lisa – your innocence, your inexperience, your trust. I've abused my son, by overlooking one very important thing – he really did love his mother, after all. I was wrong to try to play God over his future, and wrong to drag you into it. Heaven knows, none of this has been your fault. Lastly, I abused myself. I always thought, despite all my faults, that I was fundamentally honest. I wasn't. There's nothing honest about taking a sweet, naïve kid like you and bullying her into a loveless marriage.'

Every word thudded through her ribs, hammering nails into her soul.

'I just hope I haven't completely warped your attitude towards sex,' he continued. 'You're a really terrific girl, Lisa. Believe me, it's a million times better when you really love the person.'

'Love?' she challenged him, her voice oddly shrill. 'What's that?'

He looked at her sadly. 'Forget what I said about love, Lisa. It can exist, and should exist, for people like you.'

There was a long silence. Lisa's mouth had gone dry, she could not swallow. Tactfully, kindly, he was telling her to cut her losses.

'I think,' she managed to say through the lump in her throat, 'I'll go home for a holiday. Give us both time to think things over.'

He seemed relieved. 'Of course,' he said. 'Take your

171

time. Whatever you decide, of course I'll go along with it.'

'What if I decide to – stay? What about Jamie?'

'Jamie will have to adjust. If the worst comes to the worst, he can still go to boarding school.'

Alone in a first-class carriage, Lisa cried jerkily all the way to Inverness. Now that her usefulness was at an end, Michael was evidently keen to be shot of her. Even the physical bliss she had treasured had been devalued. It was a million times better, he had said, with someone you love. And he should know. If she had really wanted a truthful answer as to whether he preferred her to Barbara, she surely had it now. And not only had she deluded herself about *that*, seeing sex as a raft on which to launch her shaky marriage, she had also been fooling herself about Jamie, sentimentally fancying that this strange, challenging child felt anything but simple curiosity towards her, grossly underestimating his almost adult capacity for reproach and censure. And although Michael had never pretended to love her, she could never have envisaged him rejecting her in such a courteous, concerned, callous fashion.

Drained and devastated, she was initially glad of the comforting familiarity of Auchterbrae, nerveracking though it was having to field well-meaning enquiries from friends and neighbours. Dr Campbell, although delighted to welcome his daughter, was understandably perplexed that she should take a holiday alone so soon after her honeymoon. Lisa told him that Michael was abroad on an assignment, a story which might have satisfied him had it not been for her white face and the circles under her red-rimmed eyes. Lisa's account of Barbara's death explained away some of her obvious distress.

172

'I feel sorry for the bairn, right enough,' commented Dr Campbell. 'But he's young enough to get over it quickly, with you to help him, Lisa. A wee brother or sister is what he needs.'

After a week, she received a letter, the envelope addressed in Michael's distinctive, bold handwriting. She tore it open. Inside was the briefest of notes, and a cheque.

'I forgot to ask you if you needed any money,' the note said. 'Regards to your father. Michael.' Not 'love, Michael', of course, not even on a letter. She looked at the cheque, tears blurring the words and figures, and tossed it angrily aside.

Every morning, Lisa woke up determined to grasp the nettle and make a clean break. Clearly it was what Michael wanted. He had refused to deceive her with protestations of love, he had declared his interests right from the start, and now the motivation which would have sustained the marriage had, from his point of view, totally disintegrated. Her pride would never let her put him in the position of 'honouring his obligations to her', as he had so quaintly put it. Better no husband at all, than a reluctant one. He was right, it was wiser to pull out now before they did more lasting damage to each other, and to Jamie.

But every night, lying in her bed, racked with longing, Lisa resolved to swallow that same pride and go back to him, fight for him, hold on to her marriage for dear life, make it work. So what if he did not love her? She loved him, desperately, hopelessly. She had enough love for both of them. She was no loser − a Campbell didn't surrender the minute the going got rough. No, she wasn't giving up without a struggle. She would fight, and fight to win!

And so each day, between waking and sleeping, she

173

tore herself apart with these warring emotions – pride versus love, prudence versus courage, logic versus instinct. At the end of the second week, the telephone rang. It was Michael.

'How are you, Lisa?' His voice was solicitous but stern, clear as a bell over the five hundred miles which separated them.

'I'm fine, thank you. How are you?'

'So-so. Shall we cut the small talk now? I don't want to hassle you, but have you decided yet what you're going to do?'

'Sorry I'm taking so long about it. Very inconsiderate of me.'

'Don't be sarcastic. I didn't phone you to have a row. I haven't heard a word from you, that's all. I'm not a bloody mind reader.'

'No need to shout!'

'I'm not shouting!' he shouted. 'If you can't be reasonable over the phone, I'll fly up there tomorrow and we'll talk properly.'

'No need,' Lisa found herself saying loftily. 'Just put all my things on the train and I'll pick them up at Inverness. Goodbye, Michael.' Trembling all over, she hung up. She sat by the phone, waiting for him to ring back. But he didn't.

Dr Campbell was, mercifully, out on his rounds when Michael turned up on the doorstep the next afternoon. He walked past her into the hall without a word of greeting, his face grim. He looked tired, irritable. He hadn't any luggage with him. Lisa fought back the hope that he was going to force her to go back with him, announce that he had decided they should give things another try.

He looked oddly out of place in the front parlour, belonging as he did to a part of her life that had

174

completely detached her from her origins. Feeling absurd, she offered him tea, which he declined.

'What have you told your father?' he asked abruptly.

'That you're abroad on an assignment and that this is a holiday. I could hardly tell him the truth, could I? He thinks it's odd enough as it is, me being here. If I stay much longer the tongues will start wagging.'

'Your new term starts soon, doesn't it? Presumably you're intending to come back to London, whatever happens to us?'

'I suppose so. I hadn't thought about College.'

Michael sighed impatiently.

'I can't think in isolation,' blurted out Lisa. 'I have to have some idea what *you* want, before I can sort myself out!' That was dishonest of her, she thought, as she said it. She knew perfectly well what he wanted. It was pure masochism, to make him spell it out.

'What I want is neither here nor there. I told you I'd respect whatever decision you make.'

'Stop putting everything on to me, Michael, it isn't fair. You're so proud of your honesty, why don't you just come straight out and say it? That you wish you'd never married me and that now you want out?'

'Those are supposed to be your lines, not mine.'

'What if I won't say my lines?' She quailed at her own daring. 'What if I were to say, I love you, and I want to stay with you — what then?'

Michael seemed unmoved. 'Then I would say that your gullibility plus my guilt would be a pretty lousy basis for a marriage. I don't want to see you suffer, Lisa.'

His voice was kind, gentle, his message implacable. Lisa heard strange humming noises in her head, felt a horrible sensation of being sucked into a vacuum.

'I want to make this up to you, Lisa, in every way I can,' Michael went on quietly. 'I don't want you worrying

175

about money or accommodation. I don't want you making any compromises about your career. I want ...'

'Michael,' interrupted Lisa weakly, terrified that she would break down completely if he continued. 'Please wait for my father to get home and then take me back to London with you. I don't want him to know the truth, it would upset him too much, it would all be beyond him. Tomorrow, we'll decide on the details. I'll just go upstairs now and pack my things.'

Unsteadily, she climbed the stairs, her legs like lead, and just made it into the bathroom before she was violently sick.

They caught an overnight train back to London. Travelling first-class, they had separate sleeping compartments. Lisa woke early, got out of bed, and was promptly sick again. She had slept little. Half of her was planning a dignified exit from Michael's life. The other half was scheming desperate measures to keep him. Perhaps if she could get him into bed, he might weaken. After all, it was over a month now since they had ...

Her mind veered back along a route it had been avoiding for days: one that forked ominously, one that pointed to such wild hope and such dark despair, that she had turned her back on it firmly, to avoid inflicting further torment on herself. Climbing back into bed, dizzy and damp with sweat, she resorted to counting on her fingers. She had, technically at any rate, been married for six weeks. Her monthly cycle could, of course, be protesting against recent traumatic events, emotional upheaval, or those unfamiliar little pills. She had dutifully finished that ill-fated packet, and waited patiently for nature to reassert itself, but so far it hadn't. There had been so much else on her mind, she had chosen to ignore the fact. But now, with momentous decisions to

176

be taken, she compelled herself to consider the long-evaded possibility that she might be pregnant. She knew enough about the more rudimentary early symptoms to acknowledge, heart hammering, that she had several of them.

If she was pregnant, and she told Michael, she had little doubt what would happen. He would insist that they stayed together, out of a sense of guilt, duty and possessiveness. It was his child too. By all accounts, he took fatherhood far more seriously than he took marriage. A wife was a disposable commodity, but a child was a permanent fixture. He had already learnt that to his cost.

Perhaps fate had elected to make her decision for her. Fate had restored the missing motive to their marriage. Fate had given her an easy way out. Or had it? Had it?

Perhaps, a sinister voice whispered in her ear, fate is forcing your hand. Fate is giving you an instrument of blackmail. Fate is making a simple, if painful, decision into an agonisingly complex one, with far-reaching consequences stretching years into the future.

With sudden horrifying clarity, she saw history repeating itself. Michael and she, an imprudent marriage cobbled together by an innocent child, growing further and further apart. Michael powerful, determined, and as ruthless as ever. Lisa increasingly weak, broken and neurotic, the creaking timbers of her marriage splintering with incipient shipwreck. And after the shipwreck, who would salvage the child? The strongest swimmer, of course!

Lisa shuddered. The heartache she was suffering now was trivial indeed compared to the agony that lay in store for her if she followed that particular path. She would have only herself to blame, knowing what she did about Michael, Barbara and Jamie. If she left him now, as he

177

wanted her to, without revealing her secret, she would at least have part of him left, hers to keep forever. If she took the coward's way out, and stayed with him, not only would she probably still lose him in the end but she would risk losing her child as well. She had a vivid, petrifying insight into what Barbara must have suffered, remembering her vituperative, vicious predictions. 'Just wait,' she had said, 'until you have a baby. Wait, just wait.' Lisa could not shut her ears against the voice which echoed triumphantly, mockingly, from the grave. Gradually, her inner frenzy was superseded by an anguished calm.

Gathering up all her reserves of stamina and courage, she knew at last what she had to do.

Michael ranted and raved, of course, surprised and frustrated at his unprecedented inability to make her do exactly as he wanted. What he wanted was to buy her a flat, make her a monthly allowance, and set her up in business. Lisa had stood up to him with a vigour she had not known she possessed.

'I refuse to be paid off,' she had stated forcefully. 'I got myself into this mess, and I won't accept your conscience money. I can earn my own living, thank you very much.'

Her pregnancy was no longer in doubt. A while-you-wait laboratory test had quickly confirmed her suspicions. This secret knowledge somehow gave her an inner strength. It was gratifying to see Michael not getting his own way for a change; it gave her an unfamiliar sense of power. Suddenly, she felt herself his equal. And just as suddenly, he seemed to acknowledge it. Once he realised the full extent of her determination, he actually gave in, albeit with a very bad grace.

Lisa deeply regretted not being able to finish her course, but she hoped she might resume it at some future date. By Christmas, her pregnancy would be visible, and

178

she had no choice but to leave London before anyone guessed the truth. And so, for two terrible weeks, they shared the flat as strangers, sleeping in separate rooms, until Lisa had succeeded in finding herself a living-in catering job.

They were two weeks of hell. The atmosphere was so heavily charged with tension that Lisa felt it must choke her. Once or twice, when they touched each other accidentally, they recoiled as if from an electric shock, realising, as they both did, that physical contact would be their mutual undoing. Lisa, unable to look at Michael without her stomach going into tight knots of longing, simply avoided looking at him. Michael, for his part, made a point of leaving early each morning — mercifully, before the first waves of nausea hit her — but obstinately spent every evening at home, working in his studio, during which time he was inordinately ill-humoured while being, at the same time, chillingly polite.

They had finally agreed, coldly and calmly, that Lisa's new address and workplace would be private to her, in the interests of a clean break, and that she would not contact Michael after her departure, except, eventually, through his solicitors. They decided to keep Lisa's father in the dark, for the time being, while telling Michael's family, if the need arose, that she had gone to Scotland urgently to nurse him through a sudden illness. This plan was to give them both a few months' grace before they need cope with the inevitable questions and reactions of other people. By mutual consent, Lisa had not seen Jamie since the funeral. According to Michael, he was gradually getting over the shock of Barbara's death, and there seemed to be no point in confusing him by temporarily re-introducing Lisa back into his life.

The job Lisa had found was far from satisfactory, and she knew it, but it was, by force of circumstance, to be a

179

temporary one, and she had, after all, secured it under false pretences. The proprietors of the Mariners' Tavern, Southsea, would hardly have taken her on had they known of her pregnancy, but Lisa would have felt less guilty about her deception had she known that she was the only applicant prepared to accept the low wages they were offering. She calculated that she would be able to work for at least five months, and hoped to make herself indispensable enough to avoid a summary sacking once her secret was discovered. After that, she would have to rely on her savings for a bit, and if she ended up living on State benefits, well, plenty of other women had to manage like that. At a pinch, she could always return to Auchterbrae and swear her father to secrecy − a prospect which was less than reassuring. Her father would, without doubt, disapprove totally of her decision to deny Michael knowledge of his child's existence. It was idle, however, to speculate that far ahead. One day at a time, she told herself.

The Mariners' Tavern was a somewhat rundown pub-cum-restaurant, frequented by locals and by seamen going in and out of Portsmouth harbour. To help make ends meet, it did double duty during the summer months as a guest house serving the Southsea holiday trade. The catering service it provided was basic, traditional pub fare, plus buffet facilities for weddings and other functions. Mr and Mrs Vaughan, its harassed landlords, ran a very tight ship indeed, and Lisa felt sorry for Mrs Vaughan, who was obviously run off her feet trying to balance her business commitments against the demands of her three noisy school-age offspring. The Vaughans had survived so far, it seemed, by employing part-timers and casual labour to help with rush periods, but they had been let down so often that Mr Vaughan, after much arithmetic and many cross words, had finally given in to his wife and advertised for a full-time, live-in cook/relief barmaid.

Had Michael known the somewhat sordid details of this post, Lisa had no doubt he would have prevented her by force from accepting it. As it was, she led him to believe that she had landed herself a brilliant career opening with a prestige hotel 'somewhere in the Lake District'. It was the first deliberate lie she had ever told him, and she was amazed at how convincing she made it sound.

The last morning with Michael tested her resolve to the limits. Perplexed at her refusal to let him take her to Euston, he had finally ordered her a taxi, unaware, of course, that it would in fact be depositing her outside Victoria Coach Station. He insisted on waiting to see her off and heard her, for the first time, being sick in the bathroom.

'Are you all right in there?' he yelled, above the noise of the taps. Clammy and exhausted, Lisa reached for her toothbrush, leaning against the washbasin for support.

'It must have been those potted shrimps we had at dinner,' she called back. 'I've been up and down all night. Hope I didn't wake you.'

'You look terrible,' he remarked, as she toyed with her tea and toast. 'Why not ring them up and put it off for a few days? I promise not to listen in on the extension.'

'I'm okay now,' insisted Lisa. 'This has dragged on too long already.'

The entryphone buzzed to announce the arrival of the cab. Lisa stood up purposefully and smiled brightly.

'Goodbye then, Michael,' she said, fighting for control. 'No hard feelings.'

She knew he was going to kiss her goodbye, and froze her lips together in friendly impassivity. The touch of his mouth on hers tore her apart. For the first time since her

181

return, their eyes met full on. Hers green and glinting with unshed tears, brilliant with deception, shining with pain. His dark, enigmatic, penetrating, impenetrable.

'I won't ever forget you, Lisa,' he said softly. 'But I hope, in time, that you'll forget me.'

She smiled with secret, bitter-sweet irony.

'Not a chance,' she assured him.

Chapter Ten

Mrs Vaughan welcomed her with open arms and a full workload, and was more than glad to let Lisa take complete charge of her disorderly kitchen. No-one observing Lisa's outward industry and calm efficiency would have guessed at the suffering she privately endured. Mrs Vaughan was initially too preoccupied with her own concerns to be unduly curious about her new employee, who, as far as she was concerned, was a godsend, earning her meagre wages ten times over: even-tempered, willing, and firm with the children. Rather withdrawn, perhaps, and a bit vague in the mornings, but methodical and hard-working. Trade improved perceptibly, the increased appeal of the menu and the new decorative asset behind the bar drawing appreciation from locals and visitors alike. The incompetence which had so hampered Lisa's office career never beset her in the kitchen. She haggled successfully with local suppliers and was scrupulously honest behind the till. The Vaughans were quick to realise that they were actually in pocket as a result of engaging her. Meanwhile, Lisa was desperately relying on this hard-earned goodwill to stand her in good stead when she confronted them with her pregnancy.

As it happened, she didn't need to. Mrs Vaughan, thrice-pregnant herself, and more alert by the day since relieved of so many of her duties, noticed Lisa's thickening shape long before she felt it necessary to admit to her condition.

One afternoon, preparing pasties in the kitchen, she said gently, 'What happened, love? Don't tell me. When he found out you were in the family way, he didn't want to know, right?'

Lisa went pink, torn between her need for anonymity, for privacy, and an urge to confide in this well-meaning and motherly woman. She nodded, confused.

'Something like that,' she said, nervously fingering the place where her wedding ring had been. 'I'm sorry I had to deceive you, but I needed a job and somewhere to live. I'll be able to work for a long while yet, plenty of time for you to find a replacement.'

'What will you do? Got folks to go home to?'

'Yes, but I haven't told them yet. I come from a small town, I'd rather people there didn't find out. Gossip, you know. I've got savings, though. And I intend to go back to work as soon as I'm able.'

'You're a plucky kid, going it alone, aren't you? What about the fella? What was he like?'

Lisa clammed up. Wild horses wouldn't make her discuss Michael with anyone.

'Sorry, love, my big mouth. None of my business, I know. We won't tell my old man for a bit, right? See how it goes.'

Lisa smiled gratefully. 'Yes,' she nodded, 'we'll see how it goes.'

It went better than she had any right to expect. By the time Christmas came around, Mr Vaughan had accepted Lisa's situation as a fact of life. She had gradually become one of the family: helping the children with homework, getting them their tea, collecting the youngest from school. Every week, she phoned her father and

184

chatted convincingly about cookery and the London weather. Mercifully, if thriftily, he never suggested coming down south for a visit and announced his intention of spending Christmas with his sister on Skye. Sooner or later, Lisa kept reminding herself, he would have to be told the truth. Well, later, anyway.

Lisa's baby was due in mid-May, and by the end of March she was beginning to feel the strain. Not just physical fatigue, for she was strong and fit, but mental exhaustion, as she did endless sums in her head and discovered the impossibility of securing accommodation anywhere as an impecunious and heavily pregnant woman. Reluctantly, she forced herself to reconsider throwing herself on her father's mercy, knowing that he was quite likely to tear her off a strip before picking up the phone and spilling the beans to Michael. The prospect terrified her. She was sleeping badly and getting frequent headaches. Finally, defeated, she resigned herself to the inevitable and informed Margaret Vaughan that she would be leaving the following week.

'I can't pull my weight any more – literally,' she said ruefully. 'I've decided to go home and stay with my family.'

'Best place for you really, love,' agreed Margaret sagely. 'How did they take it?'

'"They" are just my father, actually. I haven't told him yet.' And then Lisa heard her voice wobble, felt her control snap, and found, to her horror, that she was weeping stormily all over her employer's floral housecoat.

Despite her protégée's incoherence, Margaret Vaughan was quick to read between the lines. Not accurately, perhaps – Lisa would have been mortified had she known that Margaret assumed her father to be a Victorian ogre and Auchterbrae a hotbed of small-town

185

nasties. Tactfully, however, she did not demand detailed reasons for Lisa's distress or dole out unwanted advice. She simply offered her free board and lodging, in exchange for minding the children, until she was fit to resume her duties after the birth.

'Plenty of room here for one more,' said Margaret cheerfully. 'Better than working elsewhere and putting the child out to be minded, isn't it?'

Lisa was speechless with relief and gratitude, which the Vaughans pooh-poohed with engaging honesty. 'It'd cost us money to let you go,' Margaret assured her. 'If we'd known you were in such a fix, we'd have suggested it before.'

A week later, the private traumas at the Mariners' Tavern receded in the face of dramatic national events. Disturbing news from the South Atlantic became a local preoccupation in the Portsmouth community, which was soon abuzz with frenzied preparation for the despatch of a massive task force to confront the Argentine invader, eight thousand miles across the sea.

'She doesn't look a bit like you, love,' remarked Margaret artlessly, as she peered into the crib and made cooing noises. 'Dark chap, was he?'

'Uh-huh,' nodded Lisa, leaning on an elbow and smiling sleepily down at her daughter. It was very unusual, the ward sister had told her, for a new baby to have such a head of hair. Black, of course. Those damn Delaney genes had done it again.

Lisa had been dreading visiting hour, all the other mothers being attended by doting husbands. Even the unmarried adolescent in the next bed was holding court to an uncomfortable-looking spotty youth.

'You won't be in here but a few days,' comforted Margaret, reading her thoughts. 'Don't keep you in half as long as they used to. 'Course, I expect they need the beds. She's got her work cut out, don't you think?' She made a face, jerking her head in the direction of the teenage couple. Lisa giggled. 'That's the ticket. Remember, "The child that is born on the Sabbath day, is bonny and blyth, and good and gay." I brought you all the Sunday papers. Full of the Falklands as usual. Tom never has that telly off these days. What are you going to call her?'

'Katherine, I think, after my mother. Kate for short.'

'Kate Delaney. Yes, that's got a nice ring to it. Well, Lisa, I can't stay. Nearly opening time. I'll pop in again tomorrow. 'Bye love. 'Bye-bye, Katie,' and Margaret went into a coda of goo-goo endearments, blowing kisses as she left the ward.

It was natural to feel depressed after having a baby. Everyone said so. She would soon get over it. She was lucky to have a perfect, healthy child and a home to take it to. She had no right to be depressed.

No-one knew how she had longed to have Michael beside her during those long, dark hours of labour. No-one realised the sudden, intense yearning she had felt to show him his newborn daughter. Not even she herself had bargained for the renewed, acute sense of loss that would overcome her when she first held her child in her arms, a constant future reminder of the man she loved. It was too late now, of course, for regrets. There could be no going back. It was the hard way she had chosen, but the only way.

Impatiently, she wiped the tears from her eyes and opened the Sunday papers. Such self-pity, she chided herself. Think of the poor women whose menfolk are fighting in the Falklands. They've got something to cry about. I should be ashamed of myself.

The centre pages were devoted to the latest

187

photographs of the fighting, graphically illustrating the reality of this distant, unexpected war. Lisa's gentle nature shrank instinctively from the horrors of battle. Sighing, she began to read the text, her ear cocked for the slightest sound from her baby, when the words on the page began to dance in front of her eyes. She blinked, and read again, 'These dramatic pictures by veteran war photographer Mike Delaney clearly show . . . '

A startled nurse saw Lisa's water jug hurtle to the floor, and sprang forward to attend her as she slumped sideways in a dead faint.

No-one, of course, could get out of her what exactly was the matter, except that she had to make an urgent phone call. They wouldn't let her get out of bed in case she fainted again, and she had to submit to interminable checks on her blood pressure, temperature and pulse before they would agree to wheel over the telephone trolley and plug it in.

The official at the Ministry of Defence was exceedingly courteous. Although madam was not, it seemed, registered as Mr Delaney's next of kin, he felt able to tell her at this time that there was no information to indicate that he was other than safe and well. Mumbling her thanks and swallowing hard, Lisa fumbled in her diary and, with trembling fingers, started dialling Sylvia's number. If she, Lisa, was not registered as Michael's next of kin, he must surely have named his sister.

Lisa was unprepared, in her frantic state, for the blunt reception she got.

'It's a bit late in the day for you to be showing an interest, isn't it?' she asked belligerently, 'seeing as he went out on the *Hermes* five flaming weeks ago!'

'S-Sylvia, I didn't know he had gone until today. I h-haven't heard from him for months. I rang the M.O.D. and they said you were the next of kin . . . ' The cracked, unnatural quality of her voice saved her from the further recriminations Sylvia would doubtless otherwise have piled on her head.

'Look, Lisa, I still don't know what happened between you two, because Mick's as tight as a clam and wouldn't tell me a bleeding thing. "I'm off to the Falklands," he says to me one day, cool as you like. "Tell the old lady not to worry." Well I laid into him something shocking, him a married man and everything. "Don't you ever learn your lesson?" I says to him. "Haven't you got a care for that poor little wife of yours?" "Lisa and me have split up," he says, just like that. "But don't let on to Jamie yet." Then he starts giving me the name of his solicitors, in case anything happens to him, if you please. And now you ring me up and tell me you don't know nothing about it. What the hell's been going on?'

'Where's Jamie?' persisted Lisa, desperate to extract all the information she could. Sylvia sounded angry, perplexed, resentful, likely to hang up out of sheer exasperation.

'He's at Cheltenham, isn't he, learning to be a nob. Mick reckoned Mum and me were spoiling him. "Why don't you take him, then?" I said at the time. "Lisa's the one to look after him now." "Oh no," says he, "she's busy with her cookery." And there's me believing it all! Where are you, anyway?'

Kate was whimpering. 'I can't talk now, Sylvia. I'll give you a phone number where I can be reached. Promise you'll let me know straight away if you ... hear anything.' The desperate urgency of her plea finally penetrated Sylvia's outraged verbosity.

'Portsmouth?' she queried, suspiciously. 'Are you shacked up with another bloke, or what?'

'I must go,' repeated Lisa. 'Thanks, Sylvia.'

*   *   *

Margaret was understandably puzzled by Lisa's sudden, unhealthy obsession with the Falklands war. She would sit transfixed, her baby in her arms, glued to the television and radio, running downstairs to collect the morning papers as soon as they were delivered and, stranger still, jumping up to answer the phone every time it rang, although, to Margaret's certain knowledge, Lisa had not received a single personal telephone call in all the time she had been at the Mariners' Tavern.

Besides all this, Lisa was getting thinner by the day. Margaret kept nagging her to look after herself, or her milk would stop. Nodding vaguely, Lisa would eat and drink on automatic pilot, despite which she looked increasingly haggard and ill.

'Own up, Lisa,' said Margaret finally. 'The baby's father's in the Forces, that's it, isn't it? He's out there in the Falklands.'

Horrifying news from Bluff Cove was just coming through. Lisa looked up at her, her eyes huge and haunted. Tears streaming down her face, she told Margaret the truth.

It helped, having someone to share her secret with. It helped, to put on her wedding ring again. It helped, when the nightmares woke her, to be reassured, over and over again, that all would be well.

'He's not actually in the fighting, Lisa love. And he sounds like he knows how to take care of himself. Don't fret. The baby will start fretting too. He'll be home soon, you'll see. It'll all be over before much longer.'

But nothing Margaret could say could expiate Lisa's abiding, morbid sense of guilt. Michael, she was certain, would never have reverted to his former perilous trade if she had told him the truth. No longer struggling to make his name, he would not, at this stage in his career, have unnecessarily subjected a pregnant wife to possible

190

premature widowhood. If he were killed or maimed, it would be on her conscience for the rest of her life. Useless to exhort her to follow the example of the brave, long-suffering servicemen's wives who took such ordeals in their stride. None of those courageous women, reasoned Lisa, would have her husband's blood on her head. She had never, despite the agonies of recent months, known such black torment. She took cold comfort, knowing the scope of modern weaponry, in Margaret's reminders that Michael was not actually 'in the fighting'. He'd nearly got himself killed once before, hadn't he? She shuddered as she remembered those scars. His pictures continued to filter through, irrefutable, heart-stopping evidence that he had not lost his capacity for taking risks.

And so, to Lisa's tormented spirit, her crime seemed to grow more enormous by the hour. She had deprived father and daughter of their moral right to know one another, by a narrow-minded act of self-preservation. And now, despite her repentance, the chance to redeem herself might be denied her. Helpless, she could do nothing but pray. Repeatedly, she promised God that if He brought Michael back safe and well, she would never ask Him for anything, ever again.

By the time hostilities ceased, Lisa was in a state of nervous collapse. Margaret, who had been watching her young friend vigilantly for signs of a breakdown, breathed a sigh of relief when, after the absolution of the cease-fire, Lisa crawled back, tentatively, from the precipice and began gradually eating and sleeping again. At last there was a phone call from Sylvia.

'We've had a word he's coming back on the *Hermes*,' she informed Lisa briskly. 'Very convenient for you, living where you do. Assuming you'll be wanting to be there to meet him, that is. See you on the quayside, then.'

'Sylvia,' began Lisa, haltingly, 'I know this is a

191

dreadful cheek, but ... it's important I see him alone.'

'Hmmm. You realise I've got Mum dancing about wanting to come down there and give him a hero's welcome? Her and Jamie between them reckon he won the war single-handed. Are you planning on patching things up with him?'

'What happens now,' said Lisa, ashamed, her voice sinking to a whisper, 'depends on Michael.'

Sylvia's tone softened. 'All right, pet. Leave it to me. Best of luck.' And the line went dead.

A month is a long time to wait. Lisa pored over the atlas, visualising the path of the mighty warship across the endless watery miles of the Atlantic. Quite how she would confront Michael, just what she would say to him, she had not yet decided. The same old dilemmas re-presented themselves for further painful scrutiny.

He was safe and well. For the last year he had been re-building his life. He might even be involved with another woman. Just how did she expect him to feel when she turned up out of the blue to meet him, unheralded, at the quayside? Perhaps, after all, she should let sleeping dogs lie. Perhaps she should give thanks for his return and keep her guilty secret forever. It had been pure freak, his going back to war like that. It was fanciful to suppose that such a situation would ever again arise. The Falklands crisis had been totally unexpected, and photographically had presented a unique opportunity, a special challenge. Michael had already retired once from his original, uncongenial craft. God had forgiven her, Michael was alive, and there was no reason to suppose he would ever deliberately put that life in danger again.

Pondering along these lines, she began, inevitably, to get cold feet. How could she say, 'Hello, Michael, remember me? And may I introduce you to your daughter, Kate?' How was he supposed to react? Angrily, furious at

192

her deceit? Guiltily, recognising his responsibilities towards the child? Sentimentally, reacting to the prevailing post-war euphoria? Would there be recriminations, apologies, or a maudlin reconciliation? And whichever response she received, how valid could it be? She had the advantage of surprise. She had had months to consider her own feelings. He, on the other hand, would by now have come to regard his brief marriage to her as a closed chapter, an episode in his life which he would rather forget. Her unscheduled re-appearance would be about as welcome as the proverbial skeleton at the feast.

And so, initial relief gave way to renewed despair, with Lisa again in a rapidly deteriorating psychological state. The inexorable advance of the *Hermes* now seemed a threat; it seemed to move ever faster, and a week before it was due to dock, Lisa had still not reached a decision.

She was, nonetheless, uncomfortably aware that Sylvia was now in possession of her phone number and was more than likely, in her straightforward way, to tell Michael of their conversations and pass this information on to him. She could hardly run away again, she was in no position to move on from the security of the Mariners' Tavern. Better to confront Michael on her terms than chicken out and wait instead for an approach from him — or, worse, discover that he cared so little that he did not bother to contact her at all.

Lisa threw herself into her work in an attempt to anaesthetise her aching spirit. Margaret tactfully refrained from questioning her, but noticed her pallor and listlessness. She had assumed, the war over, that Lisa's state of mind would improve enormously. At first, it had done so, only to be succeeded by this inexplicable relapse. Lisa must, she thought, be torn between relief at her husband's survival and continuing resentment at his rejection of her. In her opinion, the fellow was a bad lot and Lisa was better off without him. Still, you couldn't tell her anything these days. After that initial, tearful confession, she had clammed up again.

'For goodness sake, Lisa,' said Margaret crossly one Saturday morning, 'why don't you go out for a bit and get some fresh air? I'll look after Kate for you. Take Jason into Portsmouth and help him spend that book token he got for his birthday. Make sure he buys something decent, not one of those comic books.'

Jason, Margaret's ten-year-old, overhearing this, chimed in with, 'I want that book about the Harrier Jump Jet, Mum. That's all right, isn't it?'

'Lisa will decide whether it's suitable,' responded Margaret firmly. Charles Dickens was more what she had had in mind, but none of her children showed the slightest inclination to be well read, despite the regular issue of book tokens from a well-meaning aunt.

'Come on then, Jason,' smiled Lisa, co-operatively. 'Kate's just been fed, Margaret, so she shouldn't give you any trouble.'

'You don't know how lucky you are, having such a good baby,' muttered Margaret. 'This one,' indicating Jason with a jerk of the head, 'never stopped bawling day or night. Now get out from under my feet, both of you.'

Lisa drove Jason into Portsmouth in the Vaughan's Mini-van, only half listening to his prattle. A much less sophisticated child than Jamie, he was, consequently, far less demanding company, and she was able to conduct an indulgent conversation with him without a great deal of concentration. He was doing a good P.R. job on the book he wanted, and Lisa saw no reason to dissuade him. Jason was an aircraft fiend, and it seemed pointless to make him buy a book he wouldn't read.

'You run in and see if they've got it,' she told him, stopping outside the shop, 'while I go and park the car.'

Jason darted off obediently. Lisa located a parking space and, realising that she had not been shopping for weeks, did not hasten to rejoin him,contemplating various possible purchases for the baby. Catching sight of her reflection in a shop window, she was struck, for the first time, at the change in herself. Margaret was right, she had lost a lot of weight. While other women at the baby clinic were grumbling about the difficulty of getting their figures back, Lisa had even lost the extra inches which had once earned her the adjective 'cuddly'. Though she had never been overweight, she had never been exactly slim, until now. Her once dimpled cheeks were sculpted, her eyes seemed larger, her posture prouder. Lisa was no longer just another pretty young girl. She had become, as Michael always knew she would, a beautiful woman.

The bookshop was crowded with Saturday morning browsers. Lisa hesitated at the door, peering round for Jason.

'Lisa!' she heard him call loudly from the other side of the store. He came running towards her. 'Lisa! They've got a picture of you on a big book! *And* your name!'

Lisa could not at first think what he was talking about.

'Don't be silly, Jason. Hurry up now. Have you found the book about the Harriers?' But Jason, undeterred, was already pulling her by the hand towards the far corner of the shop where, under a sign announcing 'Latest Non-Fiction', a promotional display of large, glossy books was stacked invitingly.

She gasped. The dust jacket of the large-format book portrayed, in glowing colour, a striking redhead, flame hair vivid against green grass and the white, high-necked dress. The look on her face was rapt, dreamy, undoubtedly betraying thoughts of love. But her flesh-and-blood counterpart, stunned, transfixed, had eyes only for the title. A title that leapt out of the picture, telling her, in three words, that she was not, after all, forgotten.

'Lisa, and Others,' it read, 'by Michael Delaney'.

Lisa opened the book with trembling fingers. Inside was a simple, unobtrusive dedication, one that suffused her with such joy and pain that she lost all sense of where she was, did not hear Jason's excited questions, could see nothing but the words on the page: 'To my wife'.

Her vision blurred. Jason pulled at her sleeve.

'Lisa! Is it really you?'

'It was me . . . once,' replied Lisa.

The book revitalised her failing courage. Michael, not knowing what had become of her or where she might be, wanted her to know that he still remembered her kindly. The title, and the dedication, were surely intended as a message of some kind, she thought, fighting desperately against self-deception as she tried to decode it. What message exactly? An expression of gratitude? Probably. A plea for forgiveness? Possibly. A desire for reconciliation? No, not that. That was foolishness, fancy.

They had not parted enemies, after all. He did not know of her crime. He felt, no doubt, that after all this time they could, perhaps, be friends.

The book, she discovered, had only just come out, its publication hastened, no doubt, by Howard's shrewd deduction that if Michael was going to insist on rushing off to the Falklands, his present newsworthiness might at least do his book sales some good. Lisa had not bought the book, although she had longed to possess it. She simply could not afford it. Nearly twenty pounds seemed a criminal extravagance with Kate in need of so many things.

Jason, of course, had chattered on irrepressibly to his mother about his discovery, and Lisa had been obliged to explain to Margaret, briefly, that her husband had taken several pictures of her early in their marriage and that the

196

book had been planned long before their separation. She had no choice but to take Margaret into her confidence regarding her proposed meeting with Michael, arranging that she would take care of Kate on the day the ship came in and allow Lisa the use of the car and undisturbed occupation of one of the vacant guest rooms. One of the problems had been a suitable venue for her encounter with Michael, diverting him from an immediate return to London without introducing him to her own small bedroom, cluttered as it was with incriminating evidence. It was still possible, depending on how he reacted, that she would back out of a full confession and let Kate remain a secret if it seemed, on reflection, the best thing to do.

After a restless night, Lisa woke, pulse racing, to the morning of July twenty-first, one week short of her first wedding anniversary. The scene at the quayside dismayed her when she arrived, several hours before the ship was due to dock. So many people already, so many television cameras, so much excitement, activity. How would Michael, who wasn't even expecting her, spot her in the midst of such a throng? If he was looking out for anyone, it would be for his mother and sister, not for her. She felt guilty at depriving them of this reunion with him, but reminded herself that they, after all, had seen it all before and were doubtless more phlegmatic about the hazards Michael had faced, hardened by experience and blissfully free of guilt.

Lisa, small and alone, felt increasingly helpless amongst the boisterous, excited family groupings, some with welcoming banners. He would never see her, she should have rung his London flat and arranged a civilised meeting via the trusty Ansaphone. The only thing she had going for her, she thought miserably, was her hair, visible as a beacon, but she would need to be at least a foot taller to turn it into a positive asset. This frustration tightened into a knot of despair. Hours of waiting, hours of watching the crowd grow bigger, increased her nervous tension. By the time disembarkation commenced, she concluded, hopping from foot to foot and peering through gaps in the crowd, she would be lucky to identify Michael, let alone be visible to him. Horrified, she realised that she was on the brink of tears. She blinked them back. She had vowed to herself that she would remain cool and in control. It would be pathetic to appear, after all these months, as a hysterical, gibbering wreck.

'The little lady can't see, Kevin,' she heard a gruff voice saying behind her. 'Come to meet your young man, have you, love?'

'Yes,' confirmed Lisa, preoccupied, turning to see a middle-aged man and a strapping young one looking down at her.

'Let's give you a leg up then,' he continued kindly. 'Sit on Kevin's shoulders and wave your arms about a bit. If that don't work, try taking your clothes off.' The joke was, however, well meant, as several uninhibited young women were preparing to do just that.

'Thank you,' mumbled Lisa, clambering up, suddenly joyful at being able to see high above the sea of moving heads. On impulse, she pulled the pins hastily out of her hair, letting the wind take it.

She was prepared for a long wait, for several false alarms, for viewing hundreds of identically dressed men file off the ship and into the arms of their loved ones. Settling down on Kevin's broad shoulders, shading her eyes with her hand, telling herself to stay calm, to be patient, her heart gave a sudden, violent knock as she recognised Michael, as a civilian, disembarking before the troops.

He paused for a moment, his eyes scanning the crowd. All the breath left Lisa's lungs. She wanted to shout his name, but the sight of him paralysed her, depriving her of

198

all her strength. Then, as if in slow motion, she saw him lift the camera to his eyes, ready to immortalise the expectant throng. The lens stretched out like a lifeline. She began waving her arms wildly, bouncing with agitation on her human perch and yelling 'Michael!' at the top of her voice. Undignified it may have been, but when she saw him drop the camera and start to run, she ceased to care.

And then, everything was a blur. Surrendering at last to the overpowering mood of release and elation all around her, Lisa literally fell into his arms, felt him crushing her against the rough fabric of his jacket, let the tears flow freely. They must have stood like that for several minutes, hugging one another tightly, wordlessly, before he drew back momentarily to look at her. His eyes were molten, searching into her, instantly rekindling all the glowing embers into a roaring furnace. He kissed her. Deeply, hungrily, thirstily, an emotional kiss-of-life, reviving everything in her that had sickened and all but died. Thunder roared in her head, fire raced through her veins, all five senses were bombarded with him.

When finally he released her, they were both strangely awkward, lost for words. Lisa, gulping, shuffled through her shell-shocked memory for one of her carefully rehearsed little speeches.

'I h-hope you didn't mind me meeting you,' she stammered. 'If you can ... spare the time, I thought we might go back to my place – for a chat.' The words sounded formal, incongruous, absurd, following the impetuous, torrid embrace.

'Your place? Where's that?'

'I – I live here. In Southsea ...' began Lisa, but Michael just nodded silently, picking up his camera bag and knapsack. Like her, he seemed slightly dazed.

Holding hands so as not to lose each other in the crowd,

they eventually reached the side street where Lisa had parked the car so many hours before. Only when she started the engine with shaking fingers did she realise that she was in no fit state to drive. She turned off the ignition and sat back. A few deep breaths would do it. But Michael had already got out and was walking round to the driver's seat.

'Swap,' he commanded, curtly. 'Just tell me where to go.'

A strained silence fell as she directed him towards the Mariners' Tavern. He parked abruptly in the forecourt.

'This is where you live?' he asked, unimpressed. It did, on reflection, look a bit seedy from the outside.

'I live in,' explained Lisa. 'Actually, I more or less run the place.'

'So much for the flash hotel in the Lake District. What happened? Not another sacking to add to your collection?'

This was, encouragingly, more like old times.

'You know perfectly well that that was just a blind,' she retorted, with the asperity his tone expected of her.

'Too right I do. I had private detectives combing everywhere in Cumbria for you.'

Lisa's heart jumped at the possible significance of this bald statement.

'I was worried about you,' he clarified, dishearteningly.

She got out of the car and let them both in by the back entrance, cowering slightly as she heard the sound of Kate crying in the Vaughans' flat. Michael didn't appear to notice it. He followed her up the stairs to a large room at the top of the house, rather shabby, but dusted and polished to within an inch of its life the day before.

He looked round rather disparagingly. Admittedly, it was hardly Montpelier Gardens. The virtue of this particular room was that there was somewhere to sit besides the bed — a convertible divan which was pulled out when extra sleeping accommodation was required. Lisa plugged in the electric kettle and started fiddling with cups. Struck with debilitating stage fright, all her carefully learned lines had gone straight out of her head.

'Lisa,' said Michael gently. 'You're not really going to make tea, are you?'

She hesitated, flummoxed.

'I, er, thought you'd like something before — before you went back to London,' she faltered.

'Back to London? Oh, yes. Though I must say, that bed looks very inviting. I haven't been sleeping too well lately. Diabolical contraptions, those hammocks.' His eyes mocked her confusion. She abandoned the crockery and sat down next to him.

'I've been very worried about you,' she began uncertainly.

'Good,' he responded impassively. 'I hoped you would be.'

'Pardon?'

'You don't think I went off to the bloody Falklands for my health, do you?'

'Of course I don't. You went to — '

'Get pictures. Or rather, to get my pictures in the papers. With my name, nice and large, underneath. What did you think of them, Lisa? Of course, the best ones never got past the censor. And I must admit, I missed a few good shots. I was a bit over-cautious, sign of old age. Or perhaps I was keen to get back in one piece.'

'I'm glad to hear it,' she said simply, thrown slightly by his steely tone and the hard glint in his eyes. She was not quite sure what he was driving at, her senses blunted by the rising fear that this meeting had been a mistake. As before, outside each others' arms, they were behaving like strangers.

201

'Are you really? Would you have missed me, Lisa? How can you miss someone you'd intended never to see again?' The question was a barefaced challenge, designed to force her into some declaration of her position. She shut her eyes in self-defence.

'You *can* miss someone you've decided never to see again,' she said quietly. There was a silence.

'I know you can,' he agreed. 'Believe me, I know. Why are you afraid to look at me, Lisa?'

She opened her eyes, blinking hard, and it was like waking up from blackness into blinding daylight.

'You still don't see it, do you? Though why should you? I didn't, even when it was staring me in the face.'

'See what?' Her voice was weak, faltering.

'After we split up, Lisa, I realised that, true to my vow, I hadn't issued you with any artillery. Remember?'

She remembered. Love was like a loaded gun, he had told her. Bilateral disarmament was the fringe benefit of a loveless marriage. She nodded.

'But then, of course, you didn't need artillery,' he continued. 'Not when you'd got all those Exocet missiles.' He paused. 'You're a bit slow today, aren't you?' His voice had softened, everything about it was pure provocation.

'Let's recap, jog your powers of deduction a bit. I told you why I married you, Lisa. I needed a wife, or so I thought. Not a neurotic like Barbara, and not some half-witted hussy like all the others. No, I needed a girl with a bit of spunk, good-looking but not vain, soft-hearted but not sentimental, sensible but not boring, passionate but not predatory, a good mother for Jamie and a faithful mate for me. You fitted the bill very well. Especially as you didn't love me either. That made it fairer. Love's all humbug anyway, right?'

Lisa flinched.

'Remember me explaining the decisive moment? The

202

split-second timing that freezes truth? I managed to miss every single decisive moment I ever had with you. I missed because I was fighting instinct all along the line, rationalising, justifying, analysing ... if I took pictures that way, I'd be back on a building site by now.'

He got up and paced around the cramped room like a caged panther.

'Don't blame yourself,' blurted Lisa, terrified, in her dazed state, of misinterpreting his cryptic allusions. 'I was responsible too. And neither of us thought enough about Jamie ...'

'Ah, yes, Jamie. True to the Delaney tradition, a regular little swine. Takes after me, you see. After you'd gone, we had a man to man talk. Not that he realised you'd gone, any more than anyone else did. "Son," I say to him, "what exactly have you got against Lisa?" "Nothing, Dad," he assures me. "I like her." I ought to explain, in case you don't know, that if Jamie says he likes someone, it's a really big deal. He thinks liking anybody is a bit soft. Especially anybody female — though I expect that'll change, in time.

'"That's good," I tell him, "but she thinks you don't." "Well," he replies, "we don't have to tell her yet, do we?"'

Lisa gave Michael a blurred smile of shocked enlightenment.

'It was a sort of initiation ritual he'd worked out for you, if you like. We were newly-weds. Jamie doesn't like playing gooseberry, it was bad enough with Babs and Wainwright. He knew, as he thought, when three was a crowd.'

Lisa sighed regretfully. That much, at least, she should have understood.

'He seems to be making out okay at school,' continued Michael. 'Best place for the little blighter. Keeps getting into fights, I'm told, but knowing him, he goes looking for them. The holidays are a problem, though. He thinks it's wet, the way Sylvia and Mum dote on him, and as for me, well, I always seem to be in a bad humour these days. You're very quiet,' he digressed. 'I seem to be doing all the talking. How have you been? This doesn't look like much of a career opening to me.'

Lisa hesitated. This was the moment when she ought to confess.

'I — I was ill, for a while,' she mumbled. 'I couldn't work for a few weeks. The people here were terribly kind to me. I like it here.'

'Ill? he repeated. 'Yes, of course, you've lost weight. I hope missing me didn't put you off your food. You did say you'd missed me, didn't you?' he persisted, reminding her of her imprudent admission.

'As much as you missed me,' she parried.

'It's funny,' mused Michael. 'I spend months looking for you, with no luck, and during all that time I know exactly what I'm going to say when I find you. Now you're here I can't seem to find the right words to make you get the message. Actions not words, that's me all over. Though you must give me some credit for resourcefulness in tracking you down. I figured, rightly, that the only way to pull it off was to make you come to me. The book was the original plan, of course.'

Lisa flushed. 'I've seen it,' she admitted.

He grinned. 'But while old slowcoach Howard was still agonising over what sort of paper we should use, a rather better opportunity presented itself. Pretty drastic, you'll agree, but it worked. I thought to myself, what a wonderful way to get through to that soft-hearted girl I married.'

'Michael! You don't honestly mean to say . . .'

'Oh yes I do. I always was a cold-blooded bastard, especially when it comes to getting what I want. You

204

should know that, Lisa. Remember how badly I treated you. Remember what a miserable husband I made you. I forced you to marry me and then made you regret it. Because *I* certainly regretted it — oh yes, once I realised that there was something about you I hadn't bargained for. Something that scared me half to death. Going to the Falklands didn't take half as much guts as facing up, too late, to the truth about myself and how I felt about you. For someone who thought he knew it all, I was pig-ignorant.'

Lisa looked at him dumbly, lulled by sweet music.

'I prayed you'd be on that quayside,' he went on. 'I lay on that ship every night trying to imagine it. I kept telling myself, unless she's gone to outer Mongolia, she'll have read the papers. And even if she hasn't, she'll have seen the pictures. Wherever she is. They were printed all over the world. I just had to bank on you reading the captions. I wanted you to worry yourself sick . . . '

'Well, you certainly succeeded!' burst out Lisa, reliving her weeks of torture. 'Of all the cruel, heartless, wicked things to do!'

'Be fair,' he countered swiftly. 'I had to take the risks. Not just the obvious risks, either. The risk that you wouldn't give two hoots; that you'd sit there, reading your papers in bed, and say to the guy next to you, "See this picture? I used to know the photographer. Damn fool, going out there, he deserves all he gets."'

'How dare you imply such a thing!' stormed Lisa. 'How can you suggest that I . . . that I — '

'Well, what? You weren't supposed to become a nun, you know!'

All the impetuosity in Lisa's nature came bubbling back to the surface. He was glad she'd suffered! He had planned her suffering! And when in fact she'd been carrying his child, he had assumed, in his ignorance, that she was indulging in passing liaisons with other men! Too bemused with conflicting emotions to think straight, too agitated to dissect, calmly, the meaning of what he had been saying, she jumped up.

'Before you make any more assumptions,' she declared, 'there's something I want you to know.'

'Later,' said Michael, trapping her in his arms, his mouth descending on hers. Oh, it never failed. Anger, sadness, fear, shyness, every emotion dissolved with his touch, transformed into something stronger, sweeter, more intense.

'You want it spelled out, don't you, Mrs D.?' he murmured, kissing her throat, his tongue blazing a trail of destruction. 'L-O-V-E. Love. It does exist, after all. It's for real. It's you and me. And it hurts like hell. Kiss it better, Lisa.'

'Michael, I –'

'Don't tell me you don't love me. I deserve every other kind of punishment, but not that. This is a decisive moment, Lisa. And I'm not letting this one go.'

Lisa was in agony, her joy strangled with the knowledge of her deception.

'W-wait,' she pleaded guiltily. 'There's something I haven't told you.'

He smiled, turning her knees to jelly. 'I don't want to know. Whoever it was.'

'It isn't a question of was.'

Michael stopped smiling. 'Whoever it *is*,' he said, levelly. 'I don't want to know. Unless you'd like me to tell him personally to take a running jump. You're surely not trying to tell me that you love somebody else?'

Lisa felt a sudden stirring to sweet, loving revenge.

'Actually,' she said, wriggling free and looking at him with the utmost gravity. 'I do happen to love someone else. I love you too. I love you both.'

206

Michael's face was a picture. He was going to have to learn, she thought, that he'd met his match. She took advantage of his surprise.

'I've got to go somewhere,' she announced, brandishing this coy euphemism as she slipped quickly from the room. 'Back in a jiffy,' she sang, breezily, hearing his oath of muttered exasperation as she ran down the stairs.

Margaret, looking up, saw the pale complexion flushed into life again. Lisa went purposefully over to the cot and lifted Kate out.

'I've just given her a bottle,' explained Margaret patiently, 'as you weren't back to feed her yourself.' Kate, replete and contented, was deep in her habitual afternoon sleep.

'Thanks, Margaret,' said Lisa, brightly. 'I just want to borrow her for a moment.'

Margaret swallowed her curiosity with difficulty. Having caught a glimpse of Michael arriving from a well-chosen vantage-point, she had begun to feel that perhaps he might not be such a bad sort after all.

Quiet as a mouse, Lisa crept back up the stairs, and peered into the guest room. Michael was looking out of the window with his back to her, his posture stiff, determined, angry. Silently, Lisa lowered herself on to the divan, the baby in her arms. Right on cue, Kate wriggled in her sleep and gave a little gurgle.

Very slowly, Michael turned round. Lisa found she couldn't look up at him. She kept her eyes resolutely on Kate, who had lapsed complacently back into peaceful slumber. Wordlessly, ominously so, Michael crossed the room and crouched down in front of her. Still he didn't speak. Lisa's courage began to crumble. This was the wrong way to have gone about it. She should have told him right at the start, not accepted a declaration of love

207

and then confronted him with a baby, and probably an unwanted one at that.

'I'm sorry, Michael,' she found herself gabbling. 'It just happened. I forgot to take the pills and then – '

'*You're* apologising?' he asked softly. 'To me?'

'Well, you see, the thing is, that I . . . er . . . *knew*. That is, when we split up, I knew already but I deliberately didn't tell you because it seemed like blackmail and I didn't want us to stay together just because I was pregnant and then, you know, regret it later, and so I . . .'

Michael put his finger over her lips.

'No more' he said. 'You'll wake the baby.'

Their eyes met. 'Tell me it's a girl,' he whispered.

'It's a girl.'

'Thank God for that! She might bring out the gentleman in Jamie. Give her to me.'

Confidently, he took the little bundle from her, stood up and gazed, fascinated, at his daughter for a long time.

'Let's put her back to bed, shall we?' He smiled, looking at Lisa in a way that torpedoed every last doubt still bobbing in her mind. 'Then you can start packing. But not,' he added wickedly, eyeing the bed, 'until we've had a little nap.'